A ROMAN SPELL

A ROMAN SPELL

MICHAEL HARTWIG

Herring Cove Press

Contents

Prologue and Dedication

This book is a sequel to "Oliver and Henry," published February 2021. This book stands on its own, but some of the backstory and character development are better understood by reading "Oliver and Henry" first.

This is a work of fiction. Names, characters, businesses, places, events, locales, and incidents are either the products of the author's imagination or used fictitiously.

Several years ago, I began to work on a historical novel about Rome in the 1500s. I wanted to engage my university students in ways that would be more interesting than through academic texts. The story focused on a brilliant and well-connected cardinal, Giovanni Salviati, and an artist he patronized and welcomed into his household, Francesco de' Rossi, who later became known as Francesco Salviati. I invented another central character, Lucia, whose parents died of the plague. She was a Jewish immigrant from Spain and gifted in languages, serving as Salviati's in-house scholar. She also happened to be a sorcerer and had inherited a grimoire (a book of magic) from her grandmother.

In the end, I decided to incorporate the historical tale into a modern novel. "A Roman Spell" is set in Rome and takes up some of the themes in the historical novel. It explores contemporary cultural changes around gender, sexuality, and family life by following the lives of Giancarlo and Oliver, who are a young gay couple who seek to be good parents and loving companions despite religious and cultural biases. They and their sons Luca and Francesco are connected to people in the 1500s, so the novel takes up the question of past lives. And, since Luca has psychic or magical abilities, the book grapples with models of spirituality, religion, and magic.

The modern story includes the discovery of two journals and a grimoire (a book of magic) that reference three actual historical characters of 16th century Rome. The journals and grimoire are fictitious and used as plot devices to explore themes and interactions of that epoch. While some of the characters are historical, namely Cardinal Giovanni Salviati (1490-1553), Bishop Gian Pietro Carafa - later Pope Paul IV (1476-1559), and an artist, Francesco de' Rossi - later called Francesco Salviati (1510-1563), I do not intend the depiction of these historical characters and related events to be factual. They are fictitious and products of my (the author's) imagination.

I want to thank those who have been mentors to me in the quest to make sense of spirituality, magic, and past lives.

First and foremost, I want to thank Steve Ridini, my husband and life-partner, who so enthusiastically and lovingly opened my eyes to new ways of thinking about energy and spirituality.

I want to thank those who have worked with me and taught me so much – Deb Morreale, Stephanie Grenadier, Loretta Butehorn, Lourdes Gray, and Marilyn Massad.

Special thanks to Flavia Vittucci of Rome, Italy, for reviewing the manuscript, checking grammar, correcting Italian phrases, and verifying information about historical sites and events.

Book Cover By Author – "The Capitoline Hill – Rome"

I hope you enjoy the story and gain insights from the characters.

I

Chapter One – Languages

It was a sunny day in Rome. The October air was crisp, and the sky was blue. Oliver was taking his son for a walk in Trastevere, a historic neighborhood across the Tiber River. The area had always been a refuge for immigrants but, over the years, had become gentrified, boasting popular restaurants, clubs, galleries, and boutiques. People loved the narrow cobblestone lanes, the irregular placement of buildings, and charming open areas where people gathered to chat over coffee and drinks.

Luca was four and a half. He had inherited Oliver's blue eyes and dimples. He had a cute, round face and an affable smile that charmed everyone. They stopped at a *gelateria* just outside the Piazza di Santa Maria in Trastevere.

"*Nocciola*?" Oliver inquired, knowing Luca always chose hazelnut.

"*Sì*," Luca said enthusiastically, his eyes widening as the woman behind the counter scooped out the gelato and pressed it onto the cone.

"*Ecco*," she said as she handed the ice cream to Luca, who began to lick it avidly. Luca wore a new outfit that his two grandmothers in Boston had sent – gray cotton shorts, leather sandals, a blue sweatshirt, and a Red Sox baseball cap. Oliver placed a large paper napkin under the cone but knew it was futile; the new shirt was bound to get dripped on soon.

"What do you say?" Oliver asked his son.

"*Gracias*," Luca said without making eye contact, focused on balancing the cone in his hand.

Oliver gazed at Luca, perplexed that he had just said thanks in Spanish. He creased his forehead and watched Luca devour the gelato. Luca spoke English and Italian. Oliver wondered if Luca had just heard the Spanish word in passing. He decided to test him.

"*Quieres un café?* He asked.

Luca nodded no to the offer of a coffee in Spanish. He continued to eat his gelato with abandon. They walked down a narrow street and passed a toy store. Oliver decided to test his son again, asking if he wanted a teddy bear that was in the window. Oliver asked the question without looking at the window, as if he were simply continuing to have a casual conversation with his son as they strolled. "*Quieres este osito de peluche?*"

Luca paused, turned toward the window and then, in English, said, "I don't think so. I already have one like it."

Oliver was dumbfounded. It was one thing to use a simple word like *gracias*, particularly when it was so close to the word *grazie* in Italian. And it wasn't particularly remarkable for a kid to nod to a simple yes or no question. But his ability to comprehend Oliver's last question and respond with a complex answer seemed odd. It was unlikely he would have picked up that kind of vocabulary in passing.

Luca finished his gelato, and Oliver took his hand, leading him into the bright airy piazza. The medieval church of Santa Maria in Trastevere stood majestically over the cobblestone square. Water splashed in a small fountain where people sat on marble steps looking up at the façade of the church. It was one of the oldest churches in Rome, with foundations dating from the 4th century. The current structure was from the 12th century and boasted some of the most magnificent mosaics in the city. The façade of the church included a beautiful image of Mary holding the infant Jesus, surrounded by 10 women holding lamps. The bell in the graceful *campanile* rung twice for the hour of two.

They took a seat near the fountain and watched tourists wander through the square as they had for centuries. Music from an accordion player in front of a small café resonated off the walls of the church and the surrounding medieval structures. A couple of older boys played soccer against the left wall of the basilica. Luca seemed intrigued by their ability to pass the ball from foot to foot. Oliver leaned his head back and let the sun caress his face. He had developed an appreciation for the enchantments of Rome – leisure strolls through medieval streets, creamy gelato, abundant sunshine, and layers of history.

He nudged his son and said, "When did you learn Spanish?"

Luca looked confused.

Oliver asked in Spanish, "*Cuando aprendiste decir gracias en lugar de grazie?*" (When did you learn to say *gracias* instead of *grazie*?)

Luca shrugged his shoulders. He hesitated and then said, "It's the same thing."

Oliver was even more amazed at his son's comprehension. He asked, "I know, but when did you learn that?"

"I always knew it," Luca replied matter-of-factly.

Oliver creased his forehead. His phone pinged, and he pulled it out of his vest pocket. Giancarlo had texted: "*Ciao bello*. How are you guys doing? Do you want me to pick up anything on my way home this evening?"

Oliver replied: "We're all set. Enjoying gelato in the square. I'm preparing a caprese salad, grilled chicken, and mushroom risotto."

Giancarlo: "Sounds delicious. Do we have wine?"

Oliver: "Why don't you pick some up on your way home?"

Giancarlo: "*Va bene. Ci vediamo dopo.*"

Oliver pointed to the façade of the church and asked Luca, "Who is that at the center of the church?"

"Mary and the baby Jesus."

"Very good. And who are the others?"

"Women coming to see Jesus."

"And who are you?" Oliver asked as he pressed his forefinger playfully on the end of Luca's nose.

"Luca Russo-Monte-Fitzpatrick," Luca said proudly.

"Wow. You have a lot of names."

Luca grinned and said, "Russo is from papa and Monte-Fitz-patrick is from you, dad."

"*Bravo.*"

Luca looked back up at the façade and asked, "How come Jesus has a mother but no father?"

"Good question. He had an adoptive father – Joseph."

"How come I have two fathers but no mother?"

"Who is Maria?"

"You mean Maria, papa's sister?"

"Yeah."

"She's my godmother, my *madrina.*"

"Well, there you go. You have a godmother and two fathers."

Luca smiled, apparently satisfied with the information provided. Giancarlo's sister, Maria, offered to be a surrogate when Oliver and Giancarlo wanted to start a family. She loved being the fairy god-mother who swooped in from time to time to see Luca, but didn't have to deal with the day-to-day responsibilities of parenthood. They used Oliver's sperm. Luca inherited traits from both family lines. From Giancarlo's, Luca inherited dark hair and a tall, muscu-lar frame. He was already bigger and stronger than other boys his age. From Oliver, he inherited blue eyes, dimples, and a round face. Both Oliver and Giancarlo had dark skin tone, so Luca had a rich caramel complexion.

"Shall we go back to the house and take a siesta?"

"No. I want to play soccer," Luca said, his arms crossed in defiance.

"We'll play soccer with your cousins this weekend at the beach."

Luca smiled.

"*Andiamo*," Oliver said, taking Luca's hand and guiding him across the square into a small side street. They stopped at Aldo's produce stand, where wooden crates were stacked at the edge of the narrow street in front of a couple of motor scooters.

"*Ciao, Aldo*," Luca said gleefully, squeezing the pears in imitation of his father.

"*Ciao, Luca. Che prendete oggi?*" he asked Luca, glancing up at Oliver, who nodded to Aldo that he was looking for some fresh greens, pears, and rice.

"*Verdure e pere*," Luca said with authority.

Aldo placed a large quantity of fresh greens into a plastic bag and tied the top with a fastener, handing it to Luca. He then emptied a small basket of pears into another bag and added a package of arborio rice. Oliver handed him a 50-euro bill, and Aldo gave him change.

"*Ciao*," they all said in unison. Oliver and Luca walked a few steps farther, and Luca poked his head into Cristina's laundry shop. She waved to Luca and let him know there were things to pick up. Oliver followed Luca inside. Cristina brought out some shirts on hangers and a bag of folded clothes – underwear, shorts, and socks. Oliver paid the bill and chatted with Cristina for a while. She always had intriguing information about the comings and goings of the area.

Oliver treasured the sense of community he enjoyed in his and Giancarlo's neighborhood - the personal interaction with shopkeepers and the smells, flavors, and colors of the grocer, the butcher, the *gelateria*, and the corner café.

He and Luca continued down the street to their building,

opened the main door, and climbed the steps to the upper-level condo Giancarlo had inherited from his parents and grandparents. Oliver walked Luca up to his bedroom, removed his shoes, and laid him on the bed, tucking him under a light blanket. "*Sogni d'oro*," he wished him sweet dreams as he walked out the door.

Oliver walked back down to the parlor level, opened his computer, and checked emails. He had several new bookings for tours of ancient Rome, several messages from scholars who were proposing papers for the next symposium he was organizing around LGBTQ issues and the Church, and correspondence from his mothers – Anna and Rita – who were planning a trip in the winter when their next grandson would be born and baptized.

After doing some work, he went into the kitchen and began to prepare dinner. He picked up some ripe heirloom tomatoes from a bowl and breathed in their earthy scent. He sliced them – one red and the other yellow. He reached into the fridge for some buffalo mozzarella and began slicing it thinly, alternating the orange and red tomatoes with the velvety white cheese. He went out onto the deck to get some fresh basil and placed a few leaves artistically between the cheese and tomatoes, dressing the salad with olive oil, salt, and some dried herbs.

He then took out some chicken breasts, beat them thinly, and seasoned them with oil, mustard, herbs, and salt. He lit the gas grill on the deck and returned to the kitchen to begin the long process of making the risotto – crushing some dried porcini mushrooms, salt, herbs, and oil into a pot of arborio rice and then pouring some chicken stock and water into the pot, turning on the burner underneath.

Later, Luca wandered down from his bedroom, awakened by the aromas rising from the kitchen.

"*Vuoi un bicchiere di latte?*"

Luca nodded yes as Oliver poured him a glass of cold milk. Luca gulped it and then walked out onto the deck, peering under the lid of the grill to watch the gas flames dance underneath.

"Be careful," Oliver yelled at him. "It's hot."

Luca dropped the lid loudly and ran back into the house. He jumped into a large easy chair near the TV and clicked on the remote, finding his favorite station.

A few minutes later, Giancarlo opened the front door and came inside. Even after six years together, he still made Oliver's heart pound heavily. His trim athletic build filled his tailored jacket, and his dark skin was still tan from the summer at the beach. Oliver walked up to him and gave him a warm moist kiss, running his hands through his thick dark hair and caressing the late day stubble around his mouth and chin. "Hmm, you taste and smell so good."

"It smells heavenly in here. And how's our big boy doing today?" he inquired, walking toward Luca and picking him up off the chair, squeezing him tightly in his arms.

"We went to the square and had gelato!" Luca said excitedly.

"You did? And what else did you do?"

"We went to the market and to the bookstore."

"Not more books?" Giancarlo probed as he glared at Oliver.

Oliver glared back. "They are for Luca."

Luca leaned over and grabbed two books from the end table and held them up to Giancarlo. "*Guarda! Un libro su Castel Sant'Angelo e un altro sulla vita dei romani nell'antichità.*"

"So, are you going to be an archaeologist like your dad?" he asked, referring to the book on Castel Sant' Angelo and the other on the daily life of ancient romans.

"I want to make gelato."

"I bet you do."

Giancarlo looked at the new history books written for children and chuckled.

He took off his jacket and tie, sat down on the sofa, and opened mail. Oliver brought him a glass of wine. "Dinner will be ready in about 30 minutes. I just have to grill the chicken. The risotto is almost finished."

"Yes, I can smell it. *Porcini*, right?"

Oliver nodded. He walked out on the deck and placed the chicken breasts on the grill. As the marinade dripped onto the flames, savory smoke rose into the air. He glanced out over the courtyard lit up by a string of patio lights and waved at a neighbor across the way who was smoking a cigarette on his balcony. After a few minutes, he flipped the breasts on the grill and went back into the kitchen to check on the risotto. It was getting creamy. He added a little more chicken stock and some parmesan cheese and gave it another good stir, turning off the heat and letting it sit.

Moments later, Oliver said, "It's ready." He placed the platter of chicken and risotto near the salad on the oak table. He helped Luca onto his highchair and tucked a napkin into the collar of his shirt, placing a small piece of chicken and a portion of rice on his plate.

"Hmm, this looks delicious," Giancarlo began. He poured wine into his and Oliver's glasses and said, "*Salute!*"

"How was your day?" Oliver inquired.

"The same as usual. Nothing out of the ordinary. The market has been good, and our accounts keep growing."

"That's good news!"

"And you?" Giancarlo asked of Oliver.

"I'll share something with you later," he said, glancing toward Luca, who was pressing a spoon into the risotto.

"Another milestone?"

"More than that. Later."

Giancarlo looked worried. They continued to eat, caught up on news, and played with Luca. Once dinner was finished, Giancarlo took Luca upstairs, helped him brush his teeth, and then put him to bed, reading him a few pages from one of the new books. He returned downstairs where Oliver had finished cleaning the dishes and putting things away.

"So, what happened?"

"Well, apparently Luca speaks Spanish."

"What?" Giancarlo replied, his forehead creased.

"Yes. He said *gracias* to Bianca at the *gelateria* when she handed him his cone.

"He probably heard a tourist use the word. It's close enough to *grazie*."

"That's what I thought. But then I asked him if he wanted coffee in Spanish, and he said no. Then I asked him if he wanted a teddy bear in the window at the toy store. He pondered the question, looked at it in the window and said, 'I don't think so. I already have one like it.'"

"He said that in Spanish?"

"No, in English. But he understood my question in Spanish."

"That's strange. That kind of vocabulary is not something one would pick up off the street from tourists."

"Exactly. So, how do you think he learned it?"

"You don't think Paola has been speaking Spanish to him?"

"No. She's Italian. She's not good at other languages, remember?"

Giancarlo nodded. "Anybody else we know in the neighborhood from Spain?"

"Not that I can recall. It's strange. He seemed very comfortable with it."

"He's comfortable with languages, that's for sure. Most kids pick them up easily. But Spanish? That's odd."

"Indeed."

"By the way," Giancarlo began, "Franco and his family are going to be in San Felice Circeo this weekend. We're going, right?"

"Yes. I blocked my calendar. It's Franco's birthday, right?"

"Yes. And he's bringing the kids. They love playing with Luca," Giancarlo noted.

"And he with them."

"You up for a movie – perhaps upstairs in bed?"

"Sounds lovely," Oliver replied, raising his eyebrows playfully.

They went upstairs, poked their heads into Luca's room. He was sound asleep. They tip toed to their room. Oliver walked up to Giancarlo and began to unbutton his shirt. "I've been waiting to do this all evening."

"Hmm," Giancarlo sighed as Oliver slid his hands under the cotton fabric and caressed him. Giancarlo was well built, with broad shoulders and a well-defined chest covered in dark hair.

"Have you been working out?" Oliver inquired as he ran his hand around the edges of Giancarlo's pecs.

Giancarlo nodded. He gave Oliver a kiss, playfully exploring the wetness of his mouth.

"I still remember when Henry wanted to introduce me to his financial advisor. I thought I was going to meet an old accountant. But, *voila*, a hunk!"

Giancarlo blushed and said, "It seems so surreal." Giancarlo could still vividly recall the day Fr. Henry brought Oliver to his apartment to discuss making Oliver the beneficiary of his estate. He had expected some middle-aged nephew, and when he saw Oliver, he recalled gasping for air. He looked like a surfer from California – wavy blonde hair, blue eyes, and tan skin. He was young and curious and fascinating.

"It does seem surreal, particularly the part about our becoming parents," Oliver mused. He kicked off his shoes and unzipped his pants, tossing them on a chair. Giancarlo took his shirt off and stepped into the bathroom to brush his teeth.

Six years ago, Oliver came to Rome as a carefree college student searching for his biological father and visiting classmates in Italy.

He discovered his father was a conservative priest in the Vatican fighting to prevent a more open approach to gay people in the Church. Over the course of a month, Oliver came out as gay, fell in love with his father's financial advisor, had to deal with his father's unexpected death, changed careers, and moved permanently to Rome. Now he was married with a son. "How did all that happen – and so quickly?" he asked himself quietly as he heard Giancarlo in the bathroom. Was it all a dream? Would he wake at some point and rediscover that he was still a naïve 20-year-old trying to figure things out?

When Giancarlo returned from the bathroom and smiled warmly at him, he knew it was not a dream. They both stripped down and slipped under the covers, feeling the warmth of their bodies pressed against each other. Oliver clicked on the TV and searched for a movie. Giancarlo looked lost in thought.

"What's up?" Oliver said to him, placing the remote down.

"It feels like a lot of things are in movement – getting Luca set up for pre-school, finding a bigger place before the new baby arrives, and things at work."

"Is it too much?"

"No. It's just a lot in general."

"Welcome to parenting. Why do you think Maria enjoys being the godmother?"

"I'm beginning to see the wisdom in her approach. I wouldn't change this for the world, but it's a lot!"

"Do you miss being single?"

Giancarlo hesitated and then said, "No. Sure, it was fun, but I prefer this. I love coming home to you and Luca, and I love our outings as a family. But I don't want to lose the spark between us. It's easy to get lost in the chores of the day. I'm married to the sexiest guy in Trastevere! I never want to take that for granted."

"Don't worry. I won't let you. By the way, you're the sexiest guy in Trastevere!"

Giancarlo reached over and pressed himself against Oliver's side. He stroked his blonde curly hair and rubbed his hands over Oliver's taut lean shoulders.

"What about you? Do you regret not dating when you first came out?"

"It's funny, everyone encouraged me not to jump into a relationship, to enjoy being a single gay man after I came out. I could see their point, but I was so in love with you, I couldn't imagine wanting to date."

"You said you were in love with me?"

"I was and still am. I would pick you out of any gay crowd today and put the moves on you."

"Even if I had a son?"

"That's part of what makes you so attractive. I love that you work out, that you're fit, that you're the classic handsome Italian man," Oliver began as Giancarlo grinned. "But when I see you pick Luca up when you come home or sit down with him on the sofa to read a book, I get aroused. It is so sexy. There's something about being part of a family that is so satisfying. I'm sure there are lots of guys who enjoy being single and hooking up, but I know a lot of them would give anything to have what we have."

"You never cease to amaze me," Giancarlo said warmly to Oliver. "What did I do to deserve you?"

"With everything gay people have been through over the ages, it's about time we found happiness and love. What you went through with your dad and what I went through with mine was horrible. We deserve a break!"

Giancarlo leaned over and gave Oliver a warm kiss.

"A movie?" Oliver asked as they pulled back slightly and gaze at each other.

"I could forego the movie for something else," Giancarlo replied, raising his brows.

"Later!" Oliver said, playfully pushing Giancarlo back.

They sat up against the pillows and looked at movie offerings, settling for a favorite romantic comedy they had seen dozens of times. In a few minutes, Giancarlo was dozing. Oliver clicked off the screen, turned toward his partner, nuzzled his face in the small of his side, and fell fast asleep.

2

Chapter Two – Parting Clouds

Oliver, Giancarlo, and Luca pulled into the driveway of the family villa in San Felice Circeo, an ocean side resort south of Rome. Luca's face was pressed against the window, eager to see his cousins. Franco, Giancarlo's cousin, waved from the balcony as they stepped out of the car and unbuckled Luca from his car seat.

"*Ciao, zio Franco,*" Luca yelled enthusiastically, waving his hands. His younger cousins ran out of the house and grabbed Luca's hand, dragging him inside, where they returned to the games they had been playing.

"How was the traffic?" Franco inquired of Oliver as he came downstairs and grabbed one of Giancarlo's bags.

"Once we got past the outer loop of Rome, it was okay. It's off season, so the roads near the coast were fine."

"You guys get settled. We have some cheese and wine on the deck," Franco added. His wife Sonia approached, giving Giancarlo and Oliver kisses on their cheeks.

"It looks like the weather is going to be a little unsettled this weekend," Sonia noted as she took one of the shopping bags Oliver handed her.

"It will be nice to just relax with you. I know Luca was looking forward to seeing his cousins," Oliver noted. "By the way, happy birthday Franco!"

"*Grazie*. I'm 39 and holding!"

Everyone chuckled. He was 41.

After getting settled, Giancarlo and Oliver stepped out on the deck where Franco and Sonia had prepared a platter of antipasti – cheeses, cold cuts, olives, and nuts. Years ago, Giancarlo's grandfather had built a family compound overlooking the sea. The villa was a few blocks up from the quaint town center that lined a beautiful, sandy beach. San Felice Circeo was situated at the edge of a nature preserve on a rocky point. There were unobstructed views of the sparkling blue sea and the jagged coastline stretching off in the distance.

Each of the three families had their own private suite and balcony with breathtaking vistas. On the ground floor was a large kitchen and parlor. Most of the time, meals were served out on the deck overlooking a pool and garden. Giancarlo felt the tension from his shoulders release as he breathed in the salty sea air, blowing gently up the hillside.

"Some wine?" Franco offered.

Oliver and Giancarlo both nodded.

"How's Maria," Sonia asked Giancarlo.

"She's good. She has three months to go. She's expecting – or rather – we're all expecting around the 20th of January."

"Another boy?" Franco sought to confirm as he poured wine into their glasses.

"Yes," Giancarlo said. "Luca is looking forward to having a little brother."

"Are you guys ready?" Sonia inquired with her brows raised.

Oliver and Giancarlo looked at each other. "Well," Giancarlo began, "we are, but we need more space. We've decided to start looking for a bigger condo."

"Are you going to sell your place?" Franco asked.

"We hate to. As you know, it was our grandparents', but we need something bigger."

Franco nodded and Sonia asked, "And Luca? How's he doing?"

"He's a handful, but so much fun. He starts pre-school in January."

"I remember when my kids went off to school. I was relieved and sad. I missed having them around."

"Well, just when he's heading off, we'll have another arriving," Oliver remarked. "We're grateful for Paola. Thanks for recommending her."

"Yes, she's a gem."

"By the way, does she speak Spanish?"

Franco and Sonia looked at each other and then turned to Giancarlo and Oliver and, in unison, said, "No. Not that we are aware of. Her English is pretty limited, and we've never been aware that she knew other languages."

"We thought the same thing," Oliver said. "The other day Luca spoke some Spanish words. We were perplexed."

"Kids can pick those things up so easily. You'd be surprised," Franco noted.

Oliver nodded, took a slice of prosciutto, and glanced down into his glass of wine, deep in thought. He wasn't convinced Luca had just picked up a few random words.

Franco turned to Giancarlo and asked, "Do you need a good agent for the house hunting?"

Giancarlo took a sip of wine and said, "No. We have someone. In fact, next week we're going to look at a place our agent thinks is perfect."

"Where?"

"In the area between the Campo de' Fiori and Piazza Venezia. It's convenient for our work."

"Wow," Sonia chimed in. "That's a great neighborhood. You guys must be doing well."

Giancarlo and Oliver looked at each other and grinned. Between the money Oliver inherited from his biological father and the estate Giancarlo took over when his parents died, they were both financially well off. Giancarlo's work as a financial advisor was lucrative, and Oliver did well as a private guide. "We seem to manage," Giancarlo noted humbly.

"What's the place like that you're going to look at? Any photos?" Franco inquired.

Giancarlo opened his phone and scrolled to a webpage. "*Ecco. Il sito della casa.*"

"*Bello! Mi piace molto il soggiorno. È spazioso,*" Franco noted.

"That was what first caught our attention," Oliver remarked about the spacious living room. "We also like the roof deck overlooking the neighborhood."

"You'll have to hurry if you like it. Things don't stay on the market long," Franco added.

Luca and his three cousins all ran onto the deck and said in unison, "Can we go to the beach?"

"Please, please," Luca pleaded with Oliver, tugging at his wrist.

"*Cinque minuti,*" Franco said, buying them a few more minutes of respite. "Why don't you change into your suits?"

The kids ran back into the house and returned minutes later with towels and suits. Oliver looked out over the horizon and noticed a bank of dark clouds gathering along the coast. He said, "Hey kids, maybe we should plan on going to the beach tomorrow. It looks like rain."

"Oh," they said sadly, walking up to the edge of the garden and looking out over the water. "We don't mind the rain. We're going to get wet anyway," one of them said.

"It's dangerous," Sonia said, holding a hand to her ear as a rumble of thunder shook the ground.

Luca's cousins ran back into the house. Luca remained at the edge of the garden, gazing out at the clouds. Giancarlo, Franco, and Sonia returned to their discussion of neighborhoods in Rome. Oliver continued to watch Luca, who was waving his hands at the clouds as if trying to move them. Oliver tugged at Giancarlo's elbow and pointed quietly to Luca, who continued to wave his hands ceremoniously toward the clouds.

As Giancarlo glanced over at his son, blue sky began to appear above the clouds. He chuckled as he watched Luca continue to wave at the clouds. Soon the beach was aglow in bright sunshine. Luca looked back at his dads and grinned. Luca's cousins ran back onto the deck and pulled their father's hands. "*Guarda.* It's sunny. Can we go to the beach?"

Franco looked over at Giancarlo and Oliver and raised his shoulders as if to ask, what do you guys think?

"I'll take them down," Oliver offered. "Why don't you continue to catch up? I need to take a walk, anyway."

They nodded.

Oliver said to the kids, "*Andiamo.* Does everyone have their flip-flops, towels, suits?"

They all nodded and ran for the front door. They headed out of the villa gate and down the windy lane toward the beach. Oliver kept glancing at the sky. The clouds continued to dissipate, and the sun became more intense. He looked over at his son, who was laughing and jostling with his cousins. He was proud of him – affable and bright. And as he recalled the image of him waving the clouds away, he realized he had quite the imagination as well.

They approached the shore, the kids threw their towels and tee-shirts at Oliver's feet, and they ran toward the clear blue water. Luca had taken lessons the last two summers and was a strong swimmer. He leaped into the water and made strokes parallel to the shore.

The kids played, and Oliver sat on the sand, letting the sun warm his face. His phone rang, and it was Rita, his mother. "Hello ma," he began.

"Oliver, how are you doing? Where are you?"

"I'm sitting on the beach in San Felice Circeo, watching Luca and his cousins swim."

"You have quite the life!"

"What's up?" he asked her.

"Just wanted to say hello. We miss you."

Rita and Anna were Oliver's adoptive mothers in Boston. They had met in college and settled in Boston, eventually adopting him. They were alarmed when Oliver wanted to find his biological father and even more alarmed when their son moved to Rome to live with Giancarlo. They traveled to Rome a couple of times a year, usually during the holidays. Over the years, they grew fond of Giancarlo and more at ease with their relationship. They were ecstatic to be grandmothers, and Rita called often to check in and see new photos of her grandson.

"I miss you, too," Oliver replied warmly. "We're looking forward to your visit in January for the birth, but if you want to come sooner, you're always welcome."

"Thanks, dear. We're both busy at work."

"Ma, when I was a boy Luca's age, did I have a vivid imagination?"

"Yes. All kids do."

"Do you recall any particular examples?"

"Well, let me think. Ah, yes. This was very curious," she began excitedly. "You were fascinated with whales. When we went to Provincetown, you always insisted on our going on whale watching cruises."

"Yes. I do recall being a pain from time to time about that."

"Well. There's more. When we were on the beach, every once-in-a-while, the whales would be close enough to the shore to see them breach or spout water."

"Yes. I remember that."

"When you were about Luca's age, you used to stand on the shoreline and look out over the horizon. You mumbled some words. It was uncanny how often the whales would show up. Anna and I used to look at each other in amazement at how you seemed to imagine the whales coming close to shore, and they did."

"Hmm. I don't remember that."

"It is quite vivid in my memory. You can ask Anna. We used to laugh about it and predict to our friends who were with us on the beach that we would see whales nearby. They always wondered how we knew."

"You're kidding," Oliver remarked.

"No. It was curious and strange and cute all at once. Why did you ask about imagination?"

"Well, Luca seems very imaginative. His talent seems to be weather."

"He must be so cute!"

"He is. But it's uncanny how he seemed to have cleared the weather today. I've seen him do it other times when he wants to go out to play and it's raining."

"Enjoy it while you can. He will grow up and grow out of it like you did."

"Did I?"

"Hmm, hum."

"Ma, I never mentioned this to you, but I used to have dreams about living in Italy."

"You did?"

"Yep. They were quite vivid. I always thought it had to do with your grandparents and the whole Italian connection we had. But, in retrospect, I wonder if it was something else."

"Like intuition?"

"Maybe. I wonder if we intuit things or if we imagine them and they come to be."

There was a long silent pause on the other end of the line and then Rita said thoughtfully, "I've wondered that, too. When I was a teenager, I never pictured being with a boy – you know, like having a steady boyfriend."

"So, you knew early on?"

"I'm not so sure about that. If someone would have asked me if I was a lesbian, I would have denied it in high school. But when I think back, what I imagined was sharing a home with another woman. I can see it plain as day in my mind. It's not so much that I was imagining something; it was more that I was sensing a direction my life must have been taking already."

"I'm still perplexed by the idea that I would have intuited living in Italy. I had never traveled to Italy, and I wasn't particularly fascinated with Italy except with the idea that your family was from here."

"Things seem to be set in motion far ahead of when we notice. It's what makes life so mysterious and wonderful," Rita remarked.

"I guess so."

"Can you send pictures of Luca?"

"Yeah. Let me take one of him swimming. There. I'll text it to you."

A few moments later, Rita said, "Ahh, he is so incredibly cute. Just like you. And he's growing up so fast."

"I know. Each day his vocabulary increases, and his mannerisms become more and more grown up."

"Enjoy it. The years pass quickly. I can't believe I'm a grandmother – and going to have another grandchild shortly. That's not possible."

"It's more impossible to believe that at 27, I will be a father of two. No one does that these days."

"Well, you did start early. We tried to stop you."

"I'm glad you weren't able to. I'm so happy."

"And we're happy for you. You better hang up and watch the kids."

"They're fine, but I probably should monitor them!"

"Ciao," Rita said.

"Bye mom. I love you."

The kids splashed and swam with great abandon. When they tired, they ran toward Oliver who threw them towels. After drying, he walked them to the *gelateria* where they all got ice cream cones. They returned to the villa where the adults were laying in chaise lounges soaking up the sun. Oliver found dry clothes for Luca and tucked him into bed for a nap. He walked out onto the pool deck and took a chair next to Giancarlo.

"*Amore*, did you see Luca earlier?"

"Yes. Hmm. He's got quite the imagination."

"What do you think, though? The clouds dissipated almost immediately."

Giancarlo mumbled nonchalantly, "*Una coincidenza.*"

Oliver thought it might be more than a coincidence, given what Rita had shared with him. He leaned back in the chair and looked up at the blue sky. He checked the weather app on his phone, which showed clouds and rain for the afternoon. He checked the radar and noticed there was rain all along the coast except for the area around San Felice Circeo. 'Amazing,' he thought to himself. 'How is that possible?'

He then said to Giancarlo, "Do Franco and Sonia have plans for dinner? Should we grill something? Looks like nice weather, after all."

"Sonia is making a salad, and Franco is making some pasta. Do you want to grill some pork chops?"

"Sounds great. I'll go to the market."

Oliver got up, picked up the car keys from the kitchen counter, and headed to town. He pulled into a parking spot near a small grocer that specialized in fresh fish and meat. He walked into the shop. The owner, Enzo, looked up and smiled. "*Oliver. Buon giorno!*"

"*Buon giorno, Enzo. Novità?*"

"Nothing much new. It's quiet this time of the year."

"Do you have any good pork chops? I need eight."

"How do these look?" Enzo inquired as he pulled a platter out from the refrigerator. The platter was full of thick cut *braciole* – juicy and pink.

"*Perfetto!*"

Enzo wrapped the pork chops in butcher paper. Oliver handed him a 100-euro bill, and Enzo gave him change. Oliver returned to the villa where the kids were watching TV and the adults were preparing dinner. Oliver unwrapped the chops and began seasoning them with fresh herbs from the garden and salt and pepper. He went out on the deck and lit the grill. A few dense clouds drifted toward the shore. Oliver looked out over the horizon and then back through the large windows into the parlor. Luca caught his eye and grinned. Oliver looked back out and the clouds thinned, a few rays of sunshine filtering through.

"Weird," he murmured to himself.

A while later, everyone was gathered at a large table on the deck. The pork chops were grilled to a nice brown color. Sonia had prepared a mound of greens with cherry tomatoes, mushrooms, and shaved fennel. Franco had tossed rigatoni in a rich pesto sauce.

"Franco, where did you get the basil? This is delicious!" Oliver remarked.

"There's an organic farm up the road. Even off-season, they have fresh herbs."

"You always put just the right amount of oil, pine nuts, and parmesan in it!"

"It was something I learned from my mom."

Like Giancarlo, Franco's parents died young. He was an only child. There were heart problems in the family, and he and Sonia made every effort to exercise and eat well. The reference to Franco's mother unsettled Oliver, who always worried about Giancarlo's health. Although he exercised and ate well, there was a lot of stress at work. Oliver glanced over at Giancarlo with apprehension.

Two of Franco's and Sonia's younger boys began to fight. Luigi took some pasta off Leo's plate. Leo threw a tantrum and yelled at Luigi. Luigi explained that Leo had taken ice cream from him earlier and that he wasn't sorry. Leo denied having committed the earlier offense. Sonia reprimanded Luigi and put more pasta on Leo's plate, but he continued to scream at Luigi.

Luca was sitting on the other side of Leo. Oliver sat at the end of the table next to Luca. He noticed his son reaching under the table and holding Leo's hand. Leo calmed down. He took a sip of water and returned to eating the pasta. Luca looked toward his cousin and then felt Oliver's stare and turned to his dad. He grinned. Oliver smiled back, masking an unsettledness about a growing number of questions he had about his son.

Everyone took a deep breath and continued eating. After dinner, the kids went to the basement to watch TV. Giancarlo and Oliver cleaned dishes while Sonia and Franco looked in on the kids. A little while later, they returned to the parlor. "Coffee?" Oliver offered.

"That would be great," Sonia stated. Franco nodded.

Oliver made them all espressos, and they sat together on the sofa.

"Luca is growing up to be such a thoughtful young boy. I don't know what it is, but he seems to have a calming effect on Leo and Luigi," Sonia remarked.

Oliver nodded and said, "It must come from Giancarlo's side of the family. He has a calming effect on me."

Franco creased his forehead and added, "Giancarlo wasn't always like that. When we were cousins playing here, he was always the trouble-maker."

"If I recall, that was your role!" Giancarlo said in retort.

"Remember when we used to put lizards in Maria's bed?" Franco mused.

"That's probably why she doesn't want to be a mother!" Giancarlo noted.

Sonia looked pensive and asked, "How is she when she visits Luca? Do you think she has any regrets not playing the role of mother?"

"I think in the beginning, she did. She came more often, and she loved to hold Luca. I think she's grown accustomed to her role as godmother. I think it's interesting she offered to have another," Giancarlo said.

"I don't want to pry, but do you think having a second child is a sign that deep down, she really wants to be a mother?" Sonia pressed further.

"It's funny you mention that. We asked her the same question," Oliver noted. "She stated more emphatically that she likes the role of godmother. I think she hopes she can spend more time with Luca as he grows older, but she said pointedly that she's not cut out to be a full-time mother for toddlers."

"Well, you guys seem suited for it. Luca seems so happy and well-adjusted," Sonia observed.

"We're lucky. He seems to come by it naturally," Giancarlo noted.

"Not everyone is convinced it's good – him having two dads. You should see the stares we get from time to time in the neighborhood," Oliver added.

"Things are changing," Franco said. "You guys are trailblazers."

"Thank you, Franco," Giancarlo said. "I don't think our parents would have been too happy."

"No. I think you're right. I miss them, but they were ball busters!"

"We're so happy our kids are close to you and Luca. They will grow up realizing that two men can make great parents and a loving couple," Sonia added.

"That's how change happens," Oliver noted. "It's a slow but organic process."

They all nodded. Giancarlo stood and said, "I think I'm going to retire."

"I'll go get Luca," Oliver said in response.

"No, feel free to stay up if you like."

"No. I'm tired, too. And I imagine tomorrow will be a busy day at the beach!"

Everyone stood and exchanged kisses. Oliver went downstairs and returned with Luca in hand. He was already dozing. He and Giancarlo walked upstairs and placed Luca in his bed. They undressed, cleaned up in the bathroom, and slipped under the covers.

Oliver tugged at the puffy pillows, wrapped his arms around them, and pushed his back up against Giancarlo's warm body. Giancarlo turned toward Oliver and wrapped his arms around him. He was still smitten with Oliver - with his dark tan skin, his curly blonde hair, and his affable smile. He nuzzled himself close to Oliver. Oliver tried to close his eyes and fall asleep, but Giancarlo seemed eager to do more.

Oliver whispered, "Luca's in here. Not now. Go to sleep."

"But we can be quiet," Giancarlo whispered back. "For old times' sake. You know how magical it was when I first brought you here?"

"Yes. You cast your spell on me. But now we are fathers – and our son is a few feet away. Quiet. Go to sleep."

Giancarlo moaned in protest. "Just let me feel you up close," he begged.

Oliver turned. He was aroused. "*Un bacio e una carezza e basta.*"

"*Ma dai*, come on. I need more than a kiss and a rub."

Oliver kissed Giancarlo and ran his hand over his shoulders, squeezing his hard biceps. Giancarlo could feel Oliver's hardness against his own, and longed to hold it and stroke it. He held it tenderly for a few moments and then embraced Oliver. He knew better than to push Oliver past his comfort zone with Luca. They kissed. Oliver turned back away from Giancarlo, and Giancarlo spooned him tightly. They both fell fast asleep.

3

Chapter Three – Home

A few days later, back in Rome, Oliver and Giancarlo were getting ready for an appointment with Lorenzo, their real estate agent. He was going to show them the condo they were considering for their move. Luca was finishing breakfast, Oliver was downing a second espresso, and Giancarlo came downstairs, adjusting his tie and looking for his briefcase.

"Are we about ready?" Giancarlo asked as he glanced at Oliver, who was lifting Luca out of his chair.

"Just a few moments," Oliver replied with a hint of frustration as he wiped his son's face and hands. "Can you take him for a second?"

Giancarlo nodded as he looked at his phone for messages, taking Luca's hand. Oliver raced upstairs, brushed his teeth, and put on a light jacket. He returned downstairs and said, *"Andiamo."*

They headed downstairs and out onto the street, busy with people making their way to work. "Shall we take a taxi?" Oliver asked.

"I don't mind the walk. Lorenzo is going to meet us at the market."

Oliver nodded. They meandered through a maze of streets and onto the Ponte Sisto, a charming narrow footbridge over the Tiber. Luca always liked to look down at the swiftly running river below, the green waters dividing around the Tiber Island downstream. He stepped on the base of the railing and leaned over, Oliver holding the back of his jacket. After a pause, they continued to the other side and made their way to the busy market at the Campo de' Fiori. Lorenzo waved to them from behind a stall of apples.

They approached him and shook hands. "Are you guys ready to see the place?" he began.

Giancarlo nodded enthusiastically. "Remind us of the dimensions again," he asked as they walked toward the southern edge of the market.

"It's 130 square meters."

"What's that in square feet?" Oliver inquired. "I always forget the conversion."

"I think it's about 1400 square feet," Lorenzo replied.

"That should be big enough," Oliver noted.

Giancarlo nodded. They all made their way through the market filled with customers picking over the rich fall harvest of pears, apples, and grapes. Luca looked over at the rabbits hanging from one stall and scrunched his nose. They continued through a small archway into a quieter neighborhood.

"It's just a few hundred meters farther," Lorenzo remarked.

"I like the area. It's close to the market, but seems quiet," Giancarlo observed.

"As you know, it's a venerable historic area. The buildings are old but, for the most part, they have been well-maintained."

They continued walking through winding narrow lanes and, all-of-a-sudden, Luca tripped on a loose cobblestone. He fell face forward, scraping his wrists and knees. He sniffled a bit, but didn't cry. Oliver lifted him up and pulled out a handkerchief from his pocket. Luca looked around – first at the ground and then at the edge of the building where he stumbled – as if he were looking for someone who had caused his fall.

Oliver said, "It was just a loose cobblestone. Are you okay?"

Luca nodded, still scrutinizing the place of his fall. He seemed particularly unnerved and unconvinced that a simple cobblestone had tripped him. There was a small fountain nearby. Oliver wet the cloth and wiped Luca's hands and knees. Giancarlo and Lorenzo stood nearby, discussing the specifications of the condo they were going to see. Giancarlo looked over at Oliver and Luca and, just above their heads, noticed a for-sale sign. He glanced at the building. It was a four-story historic structure that followed the curve of the small street. There was a large double wooden door wide enough for a car to enter what, he imagined, must have been a nice courtyard.

"Lorenzo, do you know anything about this place?" Giancarlo asked, pointing to the for-sale sign.

"Yes. It's a nice unit. It's more expensive than your budget, it's larger than you had envisioned, and it needs some work."

"Hmm," Giancarlo said pensively, rubbing his chin. He then looked at Oliver and said, "Is he okay?"

"Yes. We're all set. Let's go."

They continued their walk toward the unit they were to see. Luca continued to look back at the site of his fall. Lorenzo approached a building and slipped a brass key into a large wooden door, and opened it. Inside, there was a spacious foyer leading to a broad staircase. They began climbing the steps to the main floor, where Lorenzo opened another door.

"Wow!" Giancarlo said as he walked into the expansive parlor. "This is exactly what we had imagined from the photos."

"Yes. This is one of the key selling points of the unit. It would be a great place for parties!" Lorenzo remarked, winking at them.

The room had large windows facing both the courtyard and the street. The ceilings were high, and the beams were exposed and stained dark brown. The plaster walls were in great condition. The floors were dark red antique tile covered in beautiful vintage carpets.

Oliver, holding Luca, followed Giancarlo and Lorenzo into the space. He looked around and then gazed out the courtyard-facing windows. "What's that?" he inquired with alarm.

"That's the only problem with this unit. It's an adjacent building that has been neglected. Unfortunately, there's no evidence it will be addressed soon."

"That's a problem," Giancarlo murmured to Oliver as he glanced out the same window.

"Wait till you see the roof deck and other features," Lorenzo interjected quickly, trying to salvage the sale.

They walked through the rest of the home. Next to the parlor was a spacious kitchen and dining area. The kitchen had been renovated and included new appliances and a large marble counter. "There's a study on this floor," Lorenzo noted as he opened a door to a large room with a desk and bookcases.

"This would be a wonderful workspace for both of us," Oliver said. Giancarlo nodded.

They walked upstairs and explored the two large bedrooms and two baths. "Luca, what do you think? Will this bedroom be big enough for you and your brother?" Oliver asked.

Luca nodded enthusiastically.

"Do you like the master bedroom?" Giancarlo asked of Oliver as they strolled around the space.

"It's nice. But the windows open to that other building. I'm not sure that's what I want to look at each morning."

"Let me show you the terrace," Lorenzo quickly added.

They walked up a narrow set of stairs and onto a broad deck with panoramic views of the surrounding buildings, including the Victor Emmanuel monument and the Capitoline Hill. "Amazing!" Oliver exclaimed. "The views are spectacular," he said as he gazed at the imposing statues of Castor and Pollux perched on the edge of the Piazza del Campidoglio in the distance.

"Yes," Lorenzo began. "There aren't too many units that have exclusive access to a deck like this. It's magnificent. Imagine having coffee here – or perhaps a cocktail party!"

Luca walked to the edge and looked out over the rooftops. Oliver was nervous as his son leaned against the retaining wall. He walked up behind him and took hold of his collar.

They finished the tour and walked outside. "So, what did you think?" Lorenzo asked.

"It's nice. It has the room we were looking for. It's nicely done, and the roof deck is amazing. We love the neighborhood, too."

"But?" Lorenzo asked. "I detect some reservations."

"I'm not crazy about the adjoining building. That could be a long-term problem. And I was a little nervous with Luca upstairs. We will have two young boys. Is it wise to have a roof deck?" Oliver pressed, looking at Giancarlo.

Giancarlo nodded, rubbing his chin in thought. "Lorenzo, can you get us a showing of the place we saw on the way over – where Luca tripped?"

Luca's face lit up at the mention of his name and he seemed to grasp the significance of his having forced people to see something they might have overlooked.

"Let me call the listing agent." Lorenzo opened his phone and dialed a number. He turned away from Oliver and Giancarlo and spoke quietly to the agent. He then turned back toward them and asked, "Are you free now? He is available, and the owner is out."

Giancarlo and Oliver looked at each other and nodded. "I don't have an appointment at the bank until later this afternoon," Giancarlo noted.

"*Andiamo*," Lorenzo said as he led them back to the other condo.

They approached the building, and an older man waved to Lorenzo and shook his hand.

Lorenzo then began introductions. "*Patrizio - Giancarlo e Oliver.*"

"*Piacere,*" they both responded, as Patrizio extended his hand.

"*E questo è Luca.*"

"*Piacere,*" Luca said as he extended his hand to the agent in imitation of his dads.

"Let's go inside," Patrizio invited them. "The courtyard is a common area to the complex, and it is nicely maintained. It used to be a classic interior space for horses, carriages, and supplies. The well is dry and capped. One of the owners likes to garden and maintains pots of herbs and geraniums."

Luca walked up to the capped well and scrutinized it. He then walked toward a small alcove where a marble bench was set between two antique columns. He sat on the bench and leaned back against the wall, looking out at the sun filtered space and mini-cobblestone pavement as if he were at home.

"Come on, Luca. *Andiamo,*" Oliver said as Patrizio led them inside the main part of the building.

They walked up a broad marble staircase to a landing. Luca leaped up the stairs ahead of them. "Your unit is this way," Patrizio said, pointing to the left. Luca had already pivoted in that direction and looked back at the rest as they caught up to him. "The other units are higher up the staircase and around the corner."

Patrizio opened the door to the unit. Inside was a formal parlor, not unlike the one they had just seen. There were windows on both sides, smaller ones facing the street and larger ones facing the sunny courtyard. "I already like it more than the other place," Oliver whispered to Giancarlo, who nodded.

As in the earlier home, the main room had tall ceilings and exposed wooden beams. They were on what Italians called the *piano nobile.* The tile floors were in perfect shape and covered in area rugs.

The room was full of stately antique pieces, and Giancarlo realized his own furniture would fit nicely. The plaster walls were off white, and there were gray stone accents around the windows.

Luca wandered through the space with a furrowed brow. He seemed curious, looking around corners and up at the ceiling. All of them continued to walk deeper into the unit. The curve of the building gave the room a unique feeling. Around the left side was a large formal dining room and a beautiful sunny kitchen.

"Wow!" Oliver said as he walked inside. "I've never seen a kitchen with such light."

The appliances were on the inside wall, and the sink and counter faced large open windows into the courtyard. Oliver walked over to marble surface and brushed his hand over it. He imagined some pots of fresh herbs on the windowsills and prepping meals looking out into the light. Luca reached his arms up to Oliver, who lifted him up and set him on one of the stools at the counter. He smiled as he looked out the window.

"*Andiamo.* Let's see the rest of the unit." Patrizio led them through the dining room and up another staircase to the upper level. "On this floor, you have two bedrooms, two baths, and a study."

The rooms faced the interior space, and the hallway ran along the street side of the building. The first room was a study. It had a small window and an odd wall that concealed an unremarkable closet. There was a narrow door. "What's that?" Giancarlo asked.

"Looks like a storage closet," Patrizio observed. "This room needs some attention. The space isn't being used well. From time to time, you guys must work from home, right? It would make a pleasant office or study."

Giancarlo and Oliver both nodded. Luca stuck his head inside the study and took a deep breath, scrutinizing the space. Oliver felt a chill as he looked down at his son. Luca seemed uncharacteristically engaged with the house, as if he were expecting to see or recognize something.

The second room was the smaller of the two bedrooms. It had an en suite bath. Oliver asked, "Luca, what do you think of this? Would this work for you and your brother?"

He nodded pensively. "Will we have two beds or one?" he asked.

"I think two beds. When you brother is a baby, he will need a small bed. You're a big boy, now. You need a larger one!" Giancarlo noted. The room was spacious, and Oliver thought to himself it would certainly be adequate for two boys.

Patrizio smiled and said, "Let's go see the master bedroom."

They continued down the hall. They opened the door to a beautiful room that was set between the outer and inner walls, narrowing at the far end around a large king-size bed. Inside, to the left, was another door to a beautiful marble bathroom with a tub and separate shower and double vanity. Giancarlo poked his head into the bath area and grinned. "Hmm, this is very nice."

"I love the angle of the room," Oliver remarked. "It's spacious and yet, the way it narrows near the bed, it feels cozy."

Giancarlo turned toward Oliver and said, "What do you think, dear?"

"I like it. But can we afford it?"

"Lorenzo, you said this was a little outside our budget range and needed some renovation. Aside from the study, I see little that needs to be done. What's the price?"

"The owners mentioned that there's some work needed in the kitchen, too," Patrizio added. He shared the price with Giancarlo and Oliver, who glanced at each other.

"Is there a prospectus with information about the heating system, association fees, and recent inspections?" Giancarlo asked.

Lorenzo pulled a folder out of his briefcase and handed it to Giancarlo. "*Ecco.* Everything is here."

Giancarlo and Oliver looked at each other. "Can you give us a moment?" Giancarlo said to Lorenzo and Patrizio.

They nodded and left the room. Oliver held Luca's scraped hand, giving it an affectionate kiss. "What do you think?" he began.

"I love it. It feels so much better than the other place. The price is not that much higher than what we were going to pay. I can get a good rate at the bank, and we will get a good price on our place in Trastevere. And, as I look quickly at this," he said, flipping through the prospectus, "there's nothing alarming or problematic. It looks like a well-maintained building."

"I say we should go for it. What do you think, Luca?" Oliver asked, looking at his son.

Luca nodded enthusiastically.

"Maybe we can offer a slightly lower price," Giancarlo added. He walked out into the hall and spoke with Lorenzo, coaching him on what to offer the other agent.

"Giancarlo and Oliver, why don't you go about your business? Patrizio and I will talk and call you later."

"Sounds good," Giancarlo agreed.

Giancarlo gave Oliver and Luca big hugs and walked to the bank. Oliver went back home with Luca, stopping in the market to pick up some provisions for dinner. An hour later, Giancarlo called Oliver. "*Amore*, they accepted our offer! Lorenzo said the sellers were motivated. I'll work with my colleague here to arrange financing. Can you believe it?"

"This is so exciting. I love your place, our place. But we need more room, and the place felt really good to me. It had a good vibe."

"You know I don't believe in all that stuff, but I have to admit, I felt much better in it than I did in the first place. I can't put my finger on it. It felt calming."

"Agreed. And Luca seemed to like it. In fact, he seemed very much at home there," Oliver said. As he mouthed the words, the image of Luca bouncing up the stairs toward the unit came to mind, and he chuckled nervously.

"We will be able to move into it on the first of December if all the loans get approved and we sell our other place."

"That's perfect. It gives us time to get settled before the next one arrives!"

There was a protracted silence on the other end of the line.

"Are you okay?" Oliver continued.

"Yes. Sure."

"You sound hesitant."

"No, I'm fine. I'm excited for us. See you later for dinner."

"*Ciao*," Oliver replied, hanging up the phone and returning to the preparation of dinner with Luca watching TV in the parlor.

He chuckled. He had come to Rome in a cloud of ambiguity. From time to time, he wondered if he had moved too quickly but, even as he considered the question, he knew the answer would always be the same – 'I would do it all over in a heartbeat.'

He adored Giancarlo and couldn't believe they were so lucky to have a son. Being in a relationship and having a child meant one was constantly sharing power, negotiating decisions, and responding to new facets of the other's personality. It was a lot of work, but he realized it challenged him to keep growing and to discover aspects of himself that his husband and his son highlighted for him.

Now a whole new adventure was beginning – a new home and another son. He hoped Giancarlo was okay with it all. He seemed stressed and worried. As someone approaching 40, perhaps he was lamenting the passing of his youth and realizing how domestic his life was becoming. As Oliver continued to prepare dinner, he resolved to carve out time for the two of them and find ways to keep the spark of their love alive.

4

Chapter Four – Premonitions

It was the first of December, the official day of the move. Giancarlo and Oliver sold their place quickly, and movers had been packing things into boxes and padding furniture during the previous week. Since the street outside their house was narrow, movers had to cart things to a small truck a few blocks away. Luca was with Paola. Giancarlo was in Trastevere, supervising the dismantling of the old house, and Oliver was in the new place, showing movers where to place furniture and other belongings.

Giancarlo stepped onto the balcony and looked out over the large green space for one last time. He remembered playing on the balcony as a little boy when he visited his grandparents. He moved into the house when his grandparents died and his parents took over the condo. Once his parents passed, he inherited it. The space held many memories – most fond, but some troubling.

It was in this house that he first sensed he was different and that he and his father grew distant. He was an athletic and popular teenager, and few suspected he was gay, but his father sensed something and kept arranging for dates with daughters of his clients.

Things never went well, and Giancarlo realized he would have to go away to college and pursue a career in finance to keep his dad off his back. He missed his parents and wished they could have seen his family. He clung to the belief that they would have eventually embraced his relationship with Oliver and delighted in their being grandparents. He sighed deeply.

When the last crate had been removed, he swept the floors. He took one last stroll through the house, his footsteps echoing in the empty space. He turned off the lights and locked the door behind him, walking out onto the street and over the Ponte Sisto toward his new home. He bought some flowers at the market and picked up some Prosecco at a neighborhood grocer. He walked up the steps into his new home. Oliver was resting with his head on the back of the sofa. The movers had finished, and he was exhausted.

"Wow! It looks like we've lived here forever," he said as he passed through the parlor and placed the flowers on the marble counter in the kitchen. Oliver followed him. He opened the cabinet doors and noticed that Oliver had already placed glasses and plates in their respective places. "You want some Prosecco?"

"Hmm. That would be wonderful."

Giancarlo opened the bottle, poured some into long fluted glasses, and handed one to Oliver. "You'll have to show me around. I can't believe you have it all set up. Cheers!"

"Welcome home!" Oliver said as he raised his glass.

They took sips of the bubbly liquid and began walking through the house. "The movers were great. Since we had already decided where to place things, it was easy. While they moved furniture, I unpacked boxes. Most of it is finished, although you'll have to go through your clothes and organize them as you want."

"It feels great here. I thought I would be sadder to leave the other place."

"I'm sure you will miss it, but it's nice to create a home that is ours and free from some of the lingering emotions you may have had in the other place."

Giancarlo nodded pensively, giving Oliver a kiss, and taking another sip of Prosecco.

"Do you want to go out tonight?"

Oliver nodded.

Giancarlo dialed Paola. She answered and Giancarlo began, "*Paola. Ciao.* We can come get Luca in a few minutes. How's he doing?"

"He's been great. We've been reading and watching some TV. However, he seems restless, as if he senses a big change coming. How did the move go?"

"Good. Thanks. The new place is closer to you, so it will be convenient."

Giancarlo and Oliver put on jackets, walked outside, and wandered toward Paola's apartment nearby. They picked up Luca and made their way to a popular pizzeria in the neighborhood. In the back of the restaurant, the orange glow of the wood-burning oven caught Luca's eyes. He pointed excitedly at it. "Pizza," he shouted. Everyone looked up at him and smiled.

They took a table at the side of the room and ordered water, wine, salads, and pizza. "Luca, are you ready to go see your new room later?"

He nodded yes, but he looked preoccupied, fussing with the straw the waiter had brought him for his juice, and glancing furtively at a couple sitting nearby.

"Did you have a good time with Paola today?"

He nodded yes again, without elaboration.

Oliver creased his forehead and looked at his son. Luca was ordinarily talkative and enjoyed engaging with guests at nearby tables. Oliver placed his hand on Luca's forehead to see if he had a fever.

"It's normal," he murmured to Giancarlo, using his eyes to show his concern.

"Maybe he's not happy about the move," Giancarlo whispered.

"Luca, are you okay?"

He nodded again without elaboration.

"Do you feel sick?"

He nodded no, but he looked worried. He continued to glance at the table nearby, to an older couple who were enjoying a glass of wine and a crisp margherita pizza. Oliver looked over. The couple were leaning toward each other, holding hands, enjoying their dinner.

The waiter brought their pizzas. Ordinarily, Luca would have reached immediately for a slice. He sat patiently, again glancing at the couple nearby. Oliver removed a slice from the dish and placed it on Luca's plate. He began cutting some pieces for Luca. All-of-a-sudden, the woman at the nearby table screamed, "He's choking. *Aiuta!*"

Giancarlo leaped from his chair, wrapped his arms around the older man, and lifted him up from just above his navel, giving him several powerful squeezes. The man continued to choke. Giancarlo slapped him on the back a couple of times and then repeated the Heimlich maneuver. Something dislodged in his esophagus, and the man began to breathe normally.

"*Grazie,*" he said tentatively, with a raspy voice. His wife handed him a glass of water. He drank it, stroked his throat, and then looked over to Giancarlo, Oliver, and Luca and said, "Again, thanks. Sorry I caused such a disturbance."

"We're sorry for you," Oliver said solicitously. "Are you okay?"

"Yes. Thank you. I'll be fine in a moment."

The man gained composure, and his wife relaxed, taking a sip of her wine.

Oliver cut into his pizza but kept an eye on the couple. He caught their eye at some point and asked, "Where are you from?"

"I'm from here, and my wife is from England. And you?"

"Giancarlo and Luca," he nodded toward them, "are from here. I'm from Boston."

"A pleasure. Is Luca your son?"

Oliver nodded nervously, not sure what the reaction might be to their being a gay couple with a child.

"He must have sensed something," the man noted gratefully. "He kept glancing our way before I choked."

"Hmm," Oliver murmured, looking at his son and recalling his unsettledness earlier. "You're right."

Luca smiled and then reached for his pizza. He then said, "*Papà, posso avere un po' di insalata?*"

"*Certo*," Giancarlo said, putting some salad on Luca's plate.

Oliver stared at his son. Whatever had been worrying him before had passed. He was now talkative, engaging, and happy. Oliver and Giancarlo finished their pizzas and salads, wiped Luca's face and hands, and bundled him up for the walk home. They were only a few blocks from the house. They rounded the corner, pressed an electronic combination to open the courtyard door, and walked inside. Luca began immediately to climb the steps toward their unit, as if he knew the way. He waited in front of the door to their unit as Giancarlo and Oliver approached. Oliver looked at him curiously. Once inside, Luca surveyed the room inquisitively.

"What do you think, Luca?" Giancarlo asked.

He poked his head in the kitchen and then back out into the parlor, as if something were amiss. He walked around the curve of the parlor, looking carefully at the interior wall. He walked back out into the room and said, "Everything's changed."

"We know. This is a new place. It's our old furniture, but it's in a new home," Oliver explained.

Luca didn't seem convinced, shaking his head. He looked for the stairway to the second level, took it, and wandered down the hallway. Giancarlo and Oliver followed him quickly, turning on lights as they progressed through the space. He poked his head into his room and then wandered further back to the master bedroom. He walked inside, smiled, and then returned to his own. He looked around the room and creased his forehead pensively.

"Did we set this up okay?" Giancarlo asked. "We can move things around."

"*Va bene*," he said, expressing his satisfaction. "And my brother, where will he sleep?" Luca pressed.

"We'll get him a bed and set it here," Oliver said, pointing to an empty section of the room. "Is that okay?"

"I want him to be close."

"He will," Giancarlo assured him.

Luca walked back out into the hall and toward the study. He poked his head in and then stepped back out into the hallway again as if something were out of place. Oliver walked up behind him and gave him a hug. "You ready for bed soon?"

Luca nodded. Oliver walked him back to his room and showed him the bathroom and his closet. He then said, "Papa and I will be down the hall if you need us. It's a big deal to be in a new house. So, if you need us, just come down."

Oliver pulled Luca's shirt and pants off and replaced them with pajamas. He helped him brush his teeth, go to the bathroom, and then tucked him into bed. Luca then said, "Don't worry, dad. I know my way around."

Oliver creased his forehead. He then kissed Luca on the forehead and gave him a hug. He left the room, leaving the door ajar so that a little light streamed into the room. He returned to his and Giancarlo's bedroom and found Giancarlo sorting his clothes. "Are the lights off downstairs?"

Giancarlo nodded.

"You ready to go to bed?"

He nodded again. "I'm exhausted. You must be, too."

"I am. By the way, did you notice Luca this evening? He seemed very curious about the place, as if he were looking for something?"

"He's just trying to make sense of a new home. The furniture is the same, but the space is all different. He was probably just a little disoriented."

"He said something strange just now. I told him if he needed us, we were just down the hall. He said for me not to worry – that he knew his way around."

"He is trying so hard to be grown up. He doesn't want to worry us."

"Hmm," Oliver murmured to himself. He looked off into the distance and scratched his chin in thought. He felt unsettled, as if something uncanny were lurking just below the surface – as if his son were someone other than the cute, affable, and curious 4-and-a-half-year-old he knew him to be. Were the traits he observed the prelude to a gifted child for whom he would be proud or the unfolding of something frightening, dark, and troubled?

Giancarlo slipped in under the covers while Oliver went into the bathroom. Giancarlo said excitedly, "I can't believe you even made the bed. You're amazing."

Oliver poked his head out of the bathroom and said, "I was ready to move in and get settled. Christmas will be here soon and, shortly after that, our new boy. I want to make sure we're ready."

Oliver finished in the bathroom and approached the bed. On such a cold December night, it felt good to slide under the covers and press close to Giancarlo's warm skin. He loved the solidity of his body, the manly scent of his chest, and the soft hair of his legs entwined around his own.

He reached his arm over Giancarlo's chest and pulled him close.

Even though Oliver was younger, Giancarlo savored his embrace and the security he felt from his partner, lover, husband. Oliver massaged his shoulders, running his hand down along his arms and feeling the contours of his biceps.

Oliver reached around Giancarlo's waist and felt the warmth of his sex stirring even after an exhausting day. "Don't start something you can't finish," Giancarlo murmured as Oliver stroked him.

Oliver nuzzled himself into Giancarlo's back, feeling the firmness of his buttocks. Giancarlo turned and gave Oliver a long, warm, moist kiss. He reached behind Oliver and squeezed his soft skin, rubbing his hands along his upper legs. Neither had the energy or stamina after the busy day to make love, but the closeness of their skin and the firmness of their bodies semi-aroused felt good and gratifying, and it punctuated the beginning of a new adventure in a new home. They kissed and told each other good night, falling into a peaceful sleep.

5

Chapter Five – Gay Decorator

Giancarlo took Luca's coat off and stuffed his knit cap, gloves, and red plaid scarf into one of the sleeves, hanging it on the hall tree just inside the door.

"Whew, it is cold!" he exclaimed as he rubbed his hands together and approached the thermostat to kick on the heater. "Do you want some hot chocolate?" he asked Luca.

Luca nodded and ran into the kitchen, jumping up on one of the stools. Oliver followed them into the kitchen.

"Just one hot chocolate and then you are going to take your nap," Oliver said, looking sternly at Luca, who glared back at him as if he were a monster.

"I'm going to help you put things away when they come from the store," Luca retorted, referring to the items they had just purchased for the new house.

"Your papa and I can take care of things," Oliver said nonchalantly as he filled a glass with water.

"You won't know where things go," Luca said defiantly and with concern.

"Well," Oliver began, looking over at Giancarlo, who was trying to contain his laughter in the corner, "you can help us, but the delivery people won't come for another couple of hours. You can take your nap first and help us later."

"*Arrivano*," Luca corrected Oliver, announcing the imminent arrival of the delivery team.

Oliver was just about to challenge Luca when the doorbell rang. He raised his brows, looked at Giancarlo, and then made his way to the intercom. "*Pronto*," he said.

"Your delivery," a man announced. Oliver buzzed them in and walked out onto the landing at the top of the stairs to direct them.

Two young lean men stood at the bottom of the stairs with a dolly full of boxes. "Sorry we are early. We have to make another delivery on the periphery of the city and wanted to make sure you got your items sooner than later."

"Thank you. Just bring them up here and set them inside the parlor. We can take them from there."

Luca ran into the parlor and observed the men unloading the boxes. Giancarlo approached from behind, gave the men a tip, and locked the door after they left.

"Well, I'm glad they arrived early. It will give us time to arrange things," Giancarlo said.

Luca looked at them both and tugged at the top of one of the boxes to open it. "Luca, why don't you take your nap, and you can help us later?"

"No!" he said emphatically. "I know where things go."

Oliver and Giancarlo looked at each other, shrugged their shoulders, and said, "Okay, but then you take a nap!"

They had both come to the realization that Luca's self-assertion was a good thing, evidence that he was developing a will and personality and wanted to take part in things. They also knew they had to set some boundaries so that Luca would learn how to compromise.

Oliver channeled his New England roots and kept Luca on a tight leash. Luca, however, knew how to leverage Giancarlo's streak of Italian permissiveness to get what he wanted. Occasionally, Oliver would wave a wooden spoon at them both.

Luca continued to pull open the first box. It included new dinner napkins they had picked up for the table. Luca grabbed them and took them to the hutch, pulling out one of the drawers and arranging them inside.

Giancarlo searched for the new espresso machine they bought, found it, and took it into the kitchen to set it up. Oliver found the box of new wine glasses and removed the tissue paper around them, setting them on the coffee table.

Luca found the set of espresso cups and proudly took them to his papa in the kitchen. He returned to the parlor and extracted several crystal candle holders, unwrapped them, and then placed them on the dining table, opening a door in the hutch to retrieve some new tapers. Oliver looked over at him in amazement.

Oliver took the wine glasses into the kitchen and heard the hum of the espresso machine. "Did you already get it to work?" he asked Giancarlo.

Giancarlo nodded. "It's amazing. You push a button, and it grinds the coffee, presses it, and then the frothy espresso drips out of the machine into the cup. You want one?"

Oliver nodded. As Giancarlo handed him a coffee, Luca entered the kitchen with a set of wooden spoons Oliver had picked out. He climbed on one of the stools and arranged them in the stainless-steel canister. "Looks like he might have the gay decorator gene after all," Oliver whispered to Giancarlo, who chuckled.

"That looks great. Thank you, Luca," Giancarlo said. "Do you want to finish your hot chocolate?"

"Later, I have to put other things away," Luca replied as he retreated to the parlor.

Oliver arranged glasses in one of the cabinets, and Giancarlo took care of organizing coffee, coffee cups, and other accessories for the espresso machine. Oliver stretched his neck around the corner of the kitchen into the dining room and parlor to make sure Luca was okay. He was enthusiastically opening boxes, unwrapping items, and placing them in the hutch or on the table.

"Be careful of those platters," Oliver said. "Why don't you let me take care of them?"

Luca nodded as he let a heavy piece fall back into the box. Oliver walked into the parlor and unwrapped the platters, placing them on the dining table. Luca observed carefully. Oliver considered where to put them. He picked a piece up and Luca said, "That one goes over there." He pointed to a lower shelf inside an open door of the hutch. Oliver nodded and placed it.

"And that one," Luca said as Oliver picked up another, "goes in the kitchen."

"How do you know that?" Oliver inquired.

"Well, the colored ones go in here, and the white ones in the kitchen," referring to the decorative versus the plain ceramics.

Oliver chuckled. He noticed Giancarlo was leaning in the doorway, watching. Giancarlo smiled as Luca picked up another decorative platter and placed it inside the hutch.

Giancarlo and Oliver went into the kitchen with several oversized large platters. They set them on the counter and considered where to put them. Luca followed them, picked up his cup of hot chocolate, and sipped it.

"I don't know if these will fit in the cabinets. The cabinets aren't wide enough," Oliver remarked.

"Even the lower cabinets?" Giancarlo inquired.

Oliver nodded no.

Luca observed. He placed his cup of hot chocolate back on the counter and walked over to the lower cabinet on the inside wall. He opened the door and said, "They can go here."

"But it's not wide enough," Oliver reinforced his earlier comment.

Luca sighed as if impatient. He reached inside the cabinet and wrestled with the shelf. "Luca," Oliver began, "be careful. That's going to fall. We'll find another place for the large platters."

"*Ma guarda!*" Luca said with excitement as he let the shelf fall to the bottom of the cabinet. He reached his hand to the back of the cabinet and placed his fingers in two holes that appeared where the shelf had been resting. He pulled against the wood, and the back wall of the cabinet came loose, exposing a hidden space. "See. There's room."

Oliver looked at Giancarlo in disbelief. "How did he know that was there?" Oliver whispered, squatting down, and peering into the space.

"It's a place to hide money," Luca said matter-of-factly.

Oliver stood up and looked at Giancarlo, his eyes wide with amazement. "How would he know that?" Giancarlo asked Oliver. Giancarlo kneeled on the floor and peered into the space, giving his son a hug. "Are there any more secret spaces?" he murmured into Luca's ear.

Luca looked off as if in thought and then nodded no. Giancarlo stood up with Luca in his arms. He set him on the stool in front of his hot chocolate. "Why don't you finish that and then take a nap?"

Without protest, Luca sipped the warm drink and then wiped his mouth with the back of his hand, sliding off the stool and wandering to the staircase leading to the second floor. Oliver followed him, tucked him into bed, and wished him sweat dreams.

Back in the kitchen, Oliver found Giancarlo leaning deep inside the cabinet. He asked, "Did you find any money?"

"I'm still looking," he replied, laughing.

"What was that all about?" Oliver continued.

Giancarlo extracted himself from under the cabinet and sat on one of the stools. "I have no idea. We've only been here a couple of days. Except when he's napping, we are always watching him. I can't imagine when he could have discovered that."

"Me either. Although, you know kids. They can move quickly," Oliver noted.

"I know, but I think we would have noticed."

"What other explanation is there?" Oliver asked, scratching his chin.

"I don't know. Maybe we just ask him when he's up later."

Oliver nodded. He and Giancarlo finished unpacking the boxes. As Oliver flattened the last box, he creased his forehead and walked into the kitchen where Giancarlo continued to play with the new espresso machine. "By the way," Oliver began, "besides knowing about secret spaces, how did Luca know the delivery people were coming early?"

"You're right. I almost forgot. That was odd."

"He sometimes seems to know when you're about to get home and there have been times my moms call, and he will announce their call just seconds before the phone rings."

"He must have a keen sense of intuition," Giancarlo said.

"That he does, but I'm not sure that entirely explains things."

Giancarlo looked off into the distance and nodded. He turned back toward the espresso machine and played with several buttons.

Later, Luca wandered downstairs into the kitchen. Giancarlo was at the counter checking messages, and Oliver was on his computer doing work. Oliver picked Luca up and put him on his lap. "Good nap?"

Luca nodded.

"You want some juice or fruit?"

Luca nodded no. He looked around the room.

"Son, how did you know about the hidden space under the cabinet?"

"It's always been there. Didn't you know about it?"

"It's a new house. We didn't."

"It's an old house," Luca corrected him. "It's always been there."

Giancarlo looked up from his phone at Oliver, who raised his brows.

"Well, thanks for reminding us of it," Oliver said, giving his son a hug.

Luca walked into the parlor, grabbed one of his new books, and sat in one of the large chairs, thumbing the pages and looking at the colorful drawings of ancient Roman buildings.

Oliver looked proudly at his son. Over the years, Luca had showed an exceptional ability to learn. He had quickly become fluent in Italian and English. Oliver and Giancarlo used adult words when they spoke to him, and he rapidly integrated them into a growing vocabulary. He had a great disposition – affable, calm, curious, and thoughtful.

During Luca's infancy, Oliver and Giancarlo consumed countless books on parenting. What impressed Oliver most was the idea of different intelligences. Kids developed not just verbal and mathematical knowledge, but ways of processing information about emotions and nonverbal signals – so-called social intelligence. He now wondered if there weren't other intelligences or abilities, such as intuition or even psychic things.

Oliver walked up to Giancarlo and whispered, "Do you think we should get Luca tested?"

"For what?"

"Learning abilities, intelligence, things like that."

"Are you worried?"

"I don't know. I just get nervous that these things he does might be symptomatic of something we need to pay attention to."

"He's intelligent – like his dads! That's all."

"I don't know. Spanish, influencing weather, premonitions, and familiarity with the house all seem out of the ordinary, even a bit odd."

"He's just got a good imagination, that's all. That will serve him well in the future."

"I think we should pay attention and take notes."

Giancarlo seemed uninterested and continued reading the paper. Oliver returned to his computer. He typed in a search for information about psychic abilities and kids and, to his surprise, found there was a lot more information and publications about the topic than he expected. He learned that there were so-called "indigo" children, those who had a blue aura around them and possessed psychic gifts and abilities, including deep connections with past lives. He was encouraged to learn that these children were happy and well-adjusted as long as their parents affirmed their feelings and didn't shame or make fun of them. He worried Giancarlo wouldn't react well to the information. He was grateful his moms had never shamed him, and he hoped he and Giancarlo could create the same environment for their sons.

6

Chapter Six – Christmas

At the busy Roma Termini station, Giancarlo, Oliver, and Luca stepped onto their train and found the seats they had reserved. Luca proudly pulled a small suitcase behind him, while Oliver and Giancarlo lifted their larger cases into the overhead bin. "Do you want yours up here, too?" they asked Luca.

He nodded no. He seemed very protective of his suitcase, preferring to keep it close at hand. They sat in their seats and looked out on the platform as people ran to board. A few minutes later, a soft voice announced that the train was departing. Luca's face was glued to the window as the train left Termini and wove its way through the outskirts of Rome.

"When do we get there?" Oliver inquired.

"Around two."

"Are you sure Maria's okay with us staying at her place? It's a lot for three of us to show up!"

"She's ecstatic. I think she got a Christmas tree and everything."

"Luca will be excited."

Luca set a small electronic tablet on his lap and watched a video. He occasionally glanced out the window as the city of Rome receded into the background. The unremarkable suburbs gave way to farmland and picturesque villages perched high on rocky ridges. Oliver never tired of the Italian landscape - the verdant green fields, cypress-lined roads, and historic stone barns and farmhouses set under the shadows of town walls, church spires, and crumbling castles.

The fast train picked up speed in the countryside and, before long, they were in Florence. Brunelleschi's dome stood sentinel over the lively Renaissance city center that had retained its former look even if inundated with modern tourists. After a quick stop, the train continued north to Milan.

Oliver pulled out sandwiches and chips for their lunch, and Giancarlo went to the café car to get a bottle of wine. When he returned, he poured Oliver and himself a glass and said, "*Salute*! To a nice vacation and holiday!" Luca raised his juice box.

As they got closer to the city, the landscape changed. A thin layer of snow covered the fields, and the sky was overcast. "Welcome to the north," Giancarlo noted with chagrin. "I could never live here. It's too drab."

"But you're so close to the mountains."

"That's the only consolation," Giancarlo admitted as he continued to shake his head at the grayness before him.

They arrived in Milan, walked out to the square in front of the station, and picked up a taxi. Maria lived in the city center, and in a few minutes, they were standing in front of her building. "Are you excited about seeing your *madrina*?" Giancarlo asked Luca.

He jumped up and down.

"Can you punch her button?" Oliver asked Luca.

Luca stretched to reach the intercom and pressed Maria's number. She replied, "*Pronto!*"

"*Siamo arrivati*," Luca shouted.

She buzzed them in. They took the elevator to her floor, where she was standing in the door. Maria was only a few weeks from giving birth, her belly protruding far out in front of her. Luca reached up and ran his hand over her stomach and said, "Hey brother!"

They all chuckled. Maria gave Giancarlo and Oliver kisses on their cheeks. Oliver lifted Luca to give Maria a hug and kiss. "Merry Christmas, *madrina*!"

"*Buon Natale, Luca*! Come inside. You all must be tired from the journey."

They walked inside the large space. Maria had, as Giancarlo predicted, set up a live Christmas tree in one corner of the parlor. It was a slender fir tree with lots of space between branches, where she had arranged golden lights, ornaments, and red ribbon. Luca ran quickly to examine it, noting the wrapped gifts underneath.

"Maria, everything looks so festive!"

"Well, I took time off from work, so I figured I could do some decorating," she said. "Let me take your coats. Make yourselves at home. All three of you are in the back room. I hope that's okay!"

"You're very generous to accommodate us," Oliver said warmly.

"It's my pleasure. Besides, I could use a little help."

"Whatever you need," Giancarlo noted.

Giancarlo, Oliver, and Luca wheeled their suitcases to the back bedroom and then returned. Maria had set out a platter of cheese, prosciutto, and crackers on a coffee table. "Some wine? Juice?" she said, looking at Luca?

He nodded. Giancarlo went to the kitchen and opened a bottle of wine and grabbed glasses, bringing them into the parlor. "What are you drinking?" he asked Maria.

"Water is good for now."

"So, when do you come to Rome?" Giancarlo began.

"I don't want to come too early and disturb you. But I don't want to be traveling and start having contractions."

"Come whenever you want. The new place is larger. You can sleep in Luca's room on his new bed. We'll put him in the study," Giancarlo added. Luca smiled.

"You're very generous," she said.

"Are you kidding," Oliver said. "We can't thank you enough."

"How you've raised Luca is gift enough for me. I know you'll be great with the next one. They're both so lucky to have you as fathers."

"They're lucky to have you as their godmother!" Giancarlo remarked.

Maria seemed troubled.

"Are you okay?" Oliver asked.

"Yes. I just get a little melancholy. I wish I were more maternal, but I'm not."

"That's why this is perfect. Don't feel bad about it. Luca loves you. He was talking all the way here about how he couldn't wait to see you."

She smiled and took a sip of her water.

"I just hope he doesn't regret me in the future," she whispered to Giancarlo, looking over at Luca, who was rocking his legs on the edge of the chair and looking around the room.

"We won't let him!" Oliver added in a low voice.

Maria seemed unusually anxious, Oliver thought to himself. He wondered what it must be like to carry a child to term and then give it over to someone else, even if to one's brother and brother-in-law. He pondered his own biological mother, who had given him up for adoption when his biological father, a priest, was unwilling to leave his vocation to become a father. He imagined it must have been horrible for her.

Oliver was grateful that Maria was involved in Luca's life. At some point, Luca would be curious about his biological mother. He hoped Luca wouldn't go through what Oliver had in trying to make sense of his identity.

Oliver glanced over at Giancarlo. Giancarlo had bonded deeply with Luca, all his paternal instincts kicking in, even though Luca wasn't his biological son. Oliver noticed a change in Giancarlo from the beginning, an emotional transformation and shift in identity that was unshakeable.

Oliver had the advantage of having watched his mothers parent and all they went through resisting social ostracization in being two moms of an adopted child. Rome differed from Boston, and it was exceptional to cross paths with other gay families with children. As the years passed, they found it easier to feel confident about their identity and their roles as fathers.

"So, you guys are going skiing after Christmas?"

"Yes, we made reservations at a small hotel in Courmayeur. We would like to introduce Luca to skiing. He's old enough for lessons. Do you want to come?" Giancarlo offered.

"No. That would be too much for me now. But thanks!"

"Are we going out for dinner?" Giancarlo inquired.

"If you don't mind. There's a nice place just down the block – I think you remember it."

They continued visiting and then bundled up later for the short walk to the restaurant. There was a thin coating of snow and ice on the pavement. Luca found the slick sensation under his feet fascinating. He ran his hand over a small bush and gathered a handful of snow.

"He doesn't get to see snow often," Oliver remarked as he watched his son.

"He's so cute," Maria remarked. "And he's getting so grown up."

Giancarlo and Oliver both nodded.

They entered the cozy trattoria and were shown a table along the back wall. A very handsome waiter approached and winked at them as he handed out menus. Maria leaned over to Giancarlo and whispered, "Elio couldn't quit talking about you guys after you were here last time. He thinks you are such pioneers. I'm sure you've made his day coming in."

"What would you like to drink?" Elio asked, winking at Luca.

Giancarlo ordered some wine, water, and juice. Elio brought a booster seat for Luca and asked, "What is your name, young man?"

"Luca," he exclaimed proudly.

"And your dads?"

"That's Giancarlo, and he's Oliver," he said, pointing to his dads.

"*Piacere*," Elio said.

"*E questa è la mia madrina, Maria.*"

"Yes, I know your godmother well. She comes in here a lot! What would you like to eat this evening?"

Maria glanced up at Elio and said, "The usual – a pork chop and roast potatoes."

"Luca will have *ravioli di zucca*," Oliver said as he continued to review the menu for himself.

"I'll have a *cotoletta di vitello*," Giancarlo said, "*con piselli*." The waiter nodded.

"And I'll have the *osso buco con risotto*," Oliver added. "I love the way you make it here."

"Cheers!" Giancarlo said as Elio left the table, and they all raised a glass to each other. "*Buon Natale*! It's wonderful to be together."

Maria nodded, her eyes tearing up.

"So, everything going well?" Oliver inquired.

She nodded. "Yes, no problems. The doctor said everything is in perfect order. This one is larger. I'm not looking forward to that," she said, her eyes widening.

"How's your work?" Maria asked Giancarlo.

"Good. Things have slowed a bit for the holidays."

"And yours?" she asked Oliver.

"Good as well. The winter is slower, which is good with the baby's arrival. I'll be around more."

"Do you have a name in mind yet?"

Giancarlo and Oliver looked at each other and quietly said, "We're thinking 'Gino.'"

Maria smiled. "That's nice. I like it."

Luca looked over at his dads and stared at them. Oliver felt unsettled by the look.

"Are you looking forward to having a little brother?" Maria asked Luca.

He nodded, grinned, and took another sip of his juice.

Elio returned with their food. Even in the heated restaurant, abundant steam rose from the plates in the cool, damp air of Milan. Luca attacked the ravioli with zest, Oliver trying to stay one step ahead of him, cutting them in two. Maria seemed quite hungry, piercing several roast potatoes at a time, and plopping them in her mouth.

Elio returned to ask if everything was good. Giancarlo looked up at him and smiled. "Everything is perfect. Thank you, Elio."

He seemed happy to have been addressed personally. "If there's anything you need, let me know."

They finished their dinners, returned home, and retired for the night.

The next morning, Maria was at the dining room table waiting as Giancarlo, Oliver, and Luca rose and made their way into the parlor. "Coffee, juice, milk?" she asked.

Giancarlo made his way into the kitchen and made espressos. Oliver poured Luca a glass of milk. "There's cereal, bread, marmalade, and croissants on the counter," Maria added.

"How did you sleep?" Giancarlo asked her.

"Not well. I'm very uncomfortable now. But I'll manage, thank you."

"What can we do for you? What are the plans for tonight?"

"I can't manage going to church, but if you want to, that's fine. I thought we could roast a chicken and make some risotto. I'm not up for the seven-fishes thing."

"We can make dinner. I think we might like to go to church. Do they have something earlier than midnight? Maybe a children's service?"

"I think Sant'Ambrogio has an earlier vigil with a nice choir. You should check that out."

Giancarlo nodded, heading back into the kitchen to retrieve a croissant and marmalade.

Later that evening, they bundled up and made the short walk to Sant'Ambrogio. It was one of the most important historic churches in Milan, built in the 4th century by Bishop Ambrose, one of four major doctrinal thinkers or doctors of the Catholic Church. He had been a Roman governor and was acclaimed bishop during a period of intense conflict between factions within the Church. Over the years, the church building had been rebuilt and enlarged, but it kept historic elements and had an austere but pleasing interior. The church was nearly full, and they found three seats near the back. The nave was decorated in greenery, candles, and red bows. An organist was playing background music as people gathered for the service.

Oliver continued to have ambivalent feelings about the Church. After his biological father died, he used some of the estate to sponsor symposiums on LGBTQ people and the Catholic Church. The conferences were well received by the Italian public and helped advance progressive views on gender and sexuality, putting increased pressure on the hierarchy to embrace change. But little official change had occurred within the Church, and Oliver wasn't sure he wanted to submit Luca to the toxic messages from the pulpit, nor the marginalization they felt in parish settings. The church continued to teach that his and Giancarlo's relationship wasn't authentic love, and that their parenting of Luca was tantamount to abuse.

But this was Milan, and the local church leadership had a history of being progressive and welcoming. Oliver looked around the congregation and noticed more same-sex couples than usual. Milan had a large gay population – it being the center of the Italian design and fashion industry.

A young man approached the lectern and announced the beginning of the service. He welcomed everyone and wished them a merry Christmas. The first song was a classic Christmas hymn – and, as the priest and servers processed down the aisle, Oliver began to tear up. He reached down and held Luca's hand, feeling its warmth.

The story of the birth of Jesus was always enchanting, and for Oliver, it was the key to Christianity's importance – the incarnation. The basic idea that we encounter God in our humanity was the kernel of truth that kept Oliver anchored to the Church. The pastor of the historic church gave a great sermon, emphasizing precisely that point. He underscored the importance of human dignity, and that Christmas was about celebrating how God had become flesh in our own lives.

Oliver looked over at Giancarlo and Luca and felt so blessed. Indeed, he felt that God was present in them and that he had come to learn so much about love and grace through them. He reached over Luca sitting between them and placed his hand on Giancarlo's shoulder. Giancarlo glanced around nervously, but then relaxed and savored Oliver's touch. Luca looked up at his fathers, beaming their affection. He placed each of his hands on his fathers' legs. They both reached down and grabbed his hand, all three holding hands together as the service proceeded.

The choir was superb, as Maria had promised. When the service was over, they walked back to Maria's. A light snow fell. Giancarlo said to Oliver, "I think the skiing is going to be great later in the week."

As they walked into the apartment, the aromas of the roast

chicken and risotto greeted them. "Wow, it smells heavenly in here!" Oliver remarked.

"It's almost done. Can you do some finishing touches, Oliver? I think the chicken needs a little basting – and the risotto needs more liquid and stirring. I'm exhausted."

"Take a seat," Giancarlo said. "We'll finish it."

"Luca, can you come sit with *madrina* and tell her about Mass?"

Luca slid up next to Maria on the sofa, held her hand, and described the church and the music. He had been very observant and recounted the story of Jesus's birth. Maria looked over at Giancarlo and Oliver, winking at them over Luca's head.

They enjoyed dinner and, afterwards, sat around the Christmas tree and opened presents. Although Italians often exchanged gifts on Epiphany, Giancarlo and Oliver followed the American tradition of doing so on Christmas.

Luca attacked his gifts with abandon. Maria gave him an iPad already loaded with apps for games, shows, and books. His dads gave him ski clothes – a jacket, pants, helmet, gloves, and warm underwear. His grandmothers had sent gifts to Maria's house. One box was filled with watercolors, pencils, and drawing paper. The other was a backpack for his first day at pre-school.

Giancarlo and Oliver gave Maria a painting they found in a gallery in Trastevere. It was an impressionistic image of the Forum at sunset – with golden light beaming off the columns of the temple of Castor and Pollux.

Maria, in turn, gave Oliver a gift certificate to his favorite bookstore in Rome, and she gave Giancarlo a gift certificate to a men's boutique in Milan.

Oliver and Giancarlo had agreed that the new house and new items they had bought constituted their gifts to each other. After opening gifts, they relaxed on the sofa, sipped tea, brandy, and juice, and recounted stories from earlier family gatherings.

Luca tired. Oliver took him to the bedroom and tucked him in. He returned, refilled his brandy glass, and sat in front of the tree. Giancarlo and Maria had been discussing financial matters and looked over at him as he rejoined them.

"Luca seems very verbal and observant," Maria began, shifting topics.

"Yes, he's amazing," Oliver added. "He has quite the imagination," he said as he recalled his weather antics. "And he may have the gay decorator gene!"

Maria looked askance at Oliver and Giancarlo noted, "He was directing where to put things in the new house – as if he had lived there already. I have to say, his eye for where things should go was eerie."

Oliver then asked, "Maria, when Luca was visiting with you last – did you interact with any Spanish-speaking friends?"

"No. Why?"

"Well, Luca has spoken a few Spanish words lately, and we were wondering where he picked them up."

"Hmm," she mused to herself. "I don't have any Spanish-speaking friends. Do you?"

"Just me," Oliver said. "But I just speak English and Italian to him."

"You know kids. They're very precocious."

"Yes, indeed," Giancarlo remarked.

"We're so grateful for what you're doing," Oliver noted, squeezing Maria's hand warmly.

"I am happy to do it. For some reason, the idea of giving birth brings me joy and contentment, but the idea of raising children doesn't. I'm glad this works out. You guys are incredible."

Oliver and Giancarlo looked at each other. "It's been a pleasant surprise to us both. I don't think either of us envisioned this years ago," Giancarlo noted.

"Have you been seeing anyone?" Oliver asked Maria.

"Not since I became pregnant. It's not a very enticing asset to introduce to potential boyfriends."

"Will you pick that up again after the birth?" Giancarlo asked.

"I might. There's someone I've been tracking at the local café. I think he's a lawyer."

"And he's not gay? In Milan?" Giancarlo chuckled.

"No. He's glanced my direction from time to time. I can feel the chemistry."

"What if he wants kids?" Oliver asked.

"He's older. If he wanted a family, it would have already happened. He seems very into his work. That's okay with me, given my lifestyle."

Giancarlo looked over at his sister and felt compassion. Their parents had pushed her hard to get married when, in essence, she wanted to become a lawyer. As she refused proposal after proposal, their parents became increasingly agitated and critical. It was only after their death that Maria felt comfortable in her own skin and content with the choices and decisions she had made.

He realized he and his sister had to resist the script handed to them. He envied Oliver, whose mothers encouraged him to be authentic. He hoped he could do the same for Luca, whatever Luca might consider that was out of the ordinary.

"When you're ready, we're happy to meet him, verify that he's not gay, and see if he's worthy of you!"

"*Molto gentile*," she blushed. "I think I might be ready for a long-term relationship, but I want to make sure any future husband can share power and see me as an equal partner."

"Times are changing, and there are more and more men willing to enter into partnership with women. I'm sure you will find the right one," Oliver noted.

Maria smiled contently, looking toward the Christmas tree. They continued to visit and eventually retired for the evening.

7

Chapter Seven – Courmayeur

Giancarlo, Oliver, and Luca walked from their inn to the gondola station. At the base of the ski mountain, Dolonne was a historic car-free cluster of historic stone houses and barns laden with heavy snow. The sky was bright blue and fresh snow had fallen overnight. Luca wore the new ski jacket and pants he had gotten for Christmas.

Both Giancarlo and Oliver loved skiing and had been patiently waiting for the day they could introduce Luca to the sport. Although Maria was always willing to take care of Luca while they traveled, they wanted to share their passion with him.

"Are you ready for your first day of skiing?" Oliver asked Luca as they lined up in the station, waiting for their turn to enter one of the cars.

Luca nodded but seemed preoccupied with trying to get used to thick gloves, ski clothing, and helmet. They inched their way forward and, when it was their turn, stepped into the gondola and took their seats. Soon the doors closed, the mechanism gripped the cable, and they climbed the steep slope.

Luca's face was glued to the window as trees passed outside, covered in heavy snow. Giancarlo checked the vouchers on his phone for their equipment rental and texted the instructor that they would be at Plan Checrouit in a few minutes.

Giancarlo gazed at his son with pride and joy. He was excited to introduce him to skiing and hoped he liked it. His own father had taken him as a child, and it had always been a fun family outing with lots of father-son bonding on the slopes. It was disappointing, as he grew older, that they drifted apart over the growing awareness that he might be different, that he might not be straight. He hoped he could accept his son whatever developed. For the moment, he savored the wide grin on Luca's face as he watched the winter landscape pass by.

The gondola arrived at the terminus, and they stepped outside. A cluster of hotels, restaurants, and lifts were perched on a natural plateau overlooking the valley below and the majestic mountains in the near distance. Luca's eyes widened as he watched people ski down the runs, skidding to quick stops in front of them.

A tall, athletic man approached. "Giancarlo!"

"Pietro!"

"It's so good to see you after such a long time," Pietro exclaimed.

They embraced, and Giancarlo introduced everyone. "This is Oliver, and this is Luca. This is Pietro, our ski instructor!"

"*Piacere*," they all said in unison.

"You look good. Life must be nice here!" Giancarlo said, patting the instructor's shoulder affectionately.

"I understand this is your first day, young man," he said to Luca, extending his hand. Pietro had on a red jacket and black pants. He held his helmet under one arm and his dark, thick hair rustled in the breeze. He had an affable smile, with deep-set brown eyes, dark brows and lashes, and a dark tan from the mountain sun.

Luca nodded excitedly. Oliver couldn't help but chuckle at his son and at his own first impressions of the handsome Pietro who was the polar opposite of the gnarly New England teachers he had as a child.

"*Andiamo*. Let's get your equipment."

They spent the next hour trying on skis and boots. Giancarlo and Oliver were veteran skiers and had little difficulty finding what they needed. Luca was eager to dress the adult part and enjoyed the attention of the staff as they found the right size boots and had him step into the bindings of several pairs of skis. Equipped for the day, they stepped back outside and looked to Pietro for direction.

They spent a few minutes helping Luca get used to walking in the skis. Once he had mastered coordination, they took the Pra Neron lift to the top of the nearby peak, where they could take a series of easy runs back to the base. Pietro lifted Luca up when the chair came into position and skied off with him at the top.

They gathered on a flat area in the sun and paused to take in the views. Mont Blanc towered over the resort - a massive peak studded with long, flowing glaciers. Courmayeur was surrounded by several mountain ranges, and the town was nestled in a compact valley. The Alpine views were breathtaking, and Oliver pulled out his phone to take pictures of Luca and Giancarlo with the slopes in the background.

"I'll start by having Luca ski between my legs," Pietro began.

Oliver chimed in, "Can I do that, too?"

Giancarlo jabbed a ski pole at Oliver, and Pietro winked at them both. Oliver exclaimed, "Whaaat?"

"You know what? Had I known you'd be flirting with the teacher, I would have asked for Helga instead."

"When you mentioned you had a friend who was an instructor, I didn't realize it was going to be hunky Peter."

"He's cute, isn't he," Giancarlo noted as he looked down the trail at Pietro holding Luca between his legs and encouraging Luca to keep his skis parallel.

"Luca or Pietro?" Oliver asked in gest.

"Both!"

Pietro and Luca stopped to take a break. Oliver and Giancarlo skied up to them. "He seems very coordinated," Pietro began.

"He's a quick learner," Oliver remarked. Luca looked up and smiled.

"How do you like it?" Giancarlo asked Luca.

"*Fantastico!*" he said excitedly.

Pietro took Luca for another run down the slopes, guiding him between his legs. Further down, he began to let go of his hands and encouraged Luca to balance himself. They practiced a few turns and returned to the base of the lift. Over the course of an hour or two, they repeated the run several times, with Luca getting into the rhythm of the sport quickly.

"Shall we take the other gondola to the top and ski down?" Pietro asked.

Everyone nodded. They kicked off their skis, lined up at the upper mountain gondola, stepped into one of the cars, and headed up. The views from every angle were magnificent, and Luca continued to watch skiers pass below them on the trails. He was eager to mimic the adults and, before long, could ski without Pietro's help, making smooth turns and even a few tentative skid stops instead of snow plows.

Giancarlo looked at Oliver and said, "I thought it would take a lot longer for him to pick it up."

"Me, too."

"Your boy is a natural. I've never seen anyone make such quick progress. Do you want me to stay with you, or do you want to go on your own?" Pietro asked.

"Why don't you ski with us?" Oliver interjected eagerly; a sentiment not missed by Giancarlo, who glared at him. "You can show us around the resort and help coach Luca."

They took lifts to the other side of the mountain and explored a variety of trails. There was a restaurant at the bottom of the Zerotta lift where they took a break and had lunch. The sun was strong and the wind calm, so they could sit outside on the deck. A young lady came to their table to take their orders.

"So, Pietro, how did you get into ski instruction?" Oliver asked.

"My father used to bring us here all the time. I loved it and wanted to find a way to live here full time. I began giving lessons. I like it. In the summer, I lead hiking tours on the glaciers. It's a good life."

"When did you meet Giancarlo?"

"I think when you were in school in Milan, right?" he asked, looking at Giancarlo.

Giancarlo nodded, hoping Oliver wouldn't press for more information and Pietro wouldn't be too forthcoming. Giancarlo and Pietro had a few steamy weekends together before Giancarlo got cold feet and decided he wasn't ready to come out. He was still afraid of his father, and Pietro was already wanting to introduce Giancarlo to his parents.

Oliver looked at Giancarlo, noting that he was turning red in the face and shifting uncomfortably in his chair. He knew those years were not good ones for him, so he didn't press further. He noticed Pietro wore a ring. He asked, "Do you have a family here?"

Pietro hesitated and then said, "I'm not usually very forthcoming, but since you are acquaintances and certainly understand, I can be honest. I have a boyfriend. We've been together for five years. He works in a local ski shop. It's been very nice."

"Is it difficult here?" Oliver asked.

"You mean being gay?"

Oliver nodded.

"Not really. Milan is progressive, and we have a lot of gay clients. But the local population is relatively traditional, conservative, religious. We have to be discrete. We could never do what you're doing – having a kid and everything."

"Courmayeur can't be any more conservative than Rome," Giancarlo remarked. "We've learned how to navigate things despite the resistance we encounter here and there."

"I admire you. I'd love to have children."

"You'd be good with them," Giancarlo remarked. "You were gentle and encouraging of Luca."

"He's a gem! It was easy."

They all looked at Luca who was twirling a fork full of pasta and ready to put it into his mouth, indifferent to the adults around him. They finished lunch and took the lift to the top of the mountain, where they enjoyed several runs. Pietro then said, "Do you guys want to ski on your own for a while? I can take Luca for some more lessons."

Giancarlo and Oliver looked at each other, nodded, and then turned to Luca. "Would you be okay skiing with Pietro while we go ski on our own?"

Luca nodded, looking gleefully at Pietro.

"*Allora, ci vediamo quando*?" Pietro asked.

"Let's say 4 – at Plan Checrouit?"

"*Perfetto. Andiamo, Luca?*"

"*Sì, Andiamo!*" Luca said enthusiastically, squatting over his skis as if he was ready to tackle the mountain.

Oliver and Giancarlo skied off quickly toward the Zerotta lift. They enjoyed being able to ski more aggressively. Giancarlo was an excellent skier, but Oliver had learned on the slick surfaces of New England and tackled the soft snow on the Italian slopes with abandon. He made quick sharp turns, trusting the edges to grab the surface. Giancarlo stopped and watched in amazement as Oliver continued racing toward the base of the lift.

Later, they met Luca and Pietro. "How did things go?" Oliver inquired as Luca stood in the late afternoon sun.

"He's such a natural. He is skiing as if he had been skiing for years," Pietro noted. Pietro rubbed his hands affectionately on Luca's head. Luca looked up at him and his fathers and beamed.

"Takes after his papa," Giancarlo added.

Pietro wanted to say, 'and he's got your killer looks,' but restrained himself, eyeing Oliver, who seemed unusually vigilant. Their eyes connected and Pietro got the message, 'he's mine.'

"Well, young man. You ready for dinner soon?" Oliver asked.

"Can we do pizza tonight?" Luca inquired, looking up at Giancarlo, the easier of the two to persuade.

Giancarlo nodded, getting a bit of a stare from Oliver.

Giancarlo embraced Pietro. "Thanks for your work today. We're so grateful."

Pietro rubbed his hands over Giancarlo's strong back and glanced at Oliver. He reached over and gave Oliver an affectionate hug, too. "Nice to have met you."

"*Piacere mio*," Oliver replied. "*Alla prossima.*"

"Yes – I hope it's not long before we get together again. I'd like you to meet my partner."

"We would, too," Oliver added.

Luca, Oliver, and Giancarlo took the gondola to Dolonne and cleaned up before a nice dinner at the pensione. Luca convinced the hotel staff a pizza would be appreciated. They indulged him.

Later, back in their room, Luca fell quickly asleep. Oliver and Giancarlo sat on the comfortable sofa in front of the wood-burning fireplace, their faces aglow in the orange light.

"It was fun doing this," Oliver remarked, Giancarlo staring into the flames.

"Yes. We need to get away more often. I feel like our lives are becoming so regimented. It's nice to just relax and take it easy."

Oliver glanced at Giancarlo. At times he seemed inscrutable – a handsome, sexy Italian man. He was well-built with alluring features – dark wavy hair, a broad forehead, deep-set dark eyes, and angular face with a closely trimmed dark beard lining his jaw and encircling his mouth. He was playful, as he had been on the slopes. But he was prone to long periods where he was solemn and serious. Oliver felt as if there was a battle going on inside Giancarlo – a battle between the popular, gay, fun-loving man and the conventional financial planner who worked hard, played by the rules, and didn't rock the boat. He always feared Giancarlo would wake one day and feel as if he had been wrapped in a straitjacket.

Oliver reached over and unzipped Giancarlo's ski sweater, slipping his hand inside the fabric and rubbing them over Giancarlo's chest. Giancarlo moaned and slid down on the sofa, hoping this was a prelude to something more. He stared at Oliver with widening eyes.

Oliver glanced back at Luca's room, a signal for Giancarlo to get up and close the door. Giancarlo rose, glanced in on Luca, and closed the door securely. He returned to the sofa and grabbed Oliver's hand, leading him into their bedroom. Once inside, he unzipped Oliver's pants. They fell to the floor. Oliver's hardness pressed against the stretchy fabric of his thermal underwear. Giancarlo squatted down and began to tug playfully at the fabric, grazing the erection underneath.

Oliver sat down, pulling Giancarlo down with him. Giancarlo laid on top of Oliver and starred into his blue eyes. "You were so sexy out on the slopes. I wanted to eat you up!"

"Are you sure you didn't want to eat Pietro up?" Oliver asked coyly.

"No, but he was about to devour you."

"I doubt that," Oliver said humbly.

Giancarlo gave Oliver a long, moist kiss. He then began to kiss

Oliver's neck and his shoulder. He licked around Oliver's firm, lean pecs and could feel his hardness under him. Giancarlo slipped his hands under the elastic waist of Oliver's thermals and slid them off. Oliver tugged at Giancarlo's, sliding the stretchy fabric down over his shaft. In the soft light of the bedroom lamp, they faced each other in the bare nakedness of their bodies. It had been months since they had the time or leisure to take their time with each other, to bare themselves – body and soul.

They knew each other's bodies intimately – each contour and hollow. There were customary positions and places they settled into as their bodies spoke to each other. Giancarlo's legs were particularly fluent in conveying strength, power, and authority as he enfolded Oliver. Oliver's body was adept at playful resistance, inviting Giancarlo's dominion, yet pushing back, compelling him to be decisive.

Each knew the other's vulnerability and learned how to assure the other with affection, Giancarlo nibbling behind Oliver's neck, and Oliver massaging the inside of Giancarlo's legs. For Oliver, a whispered *ti voglio bene* in his ear not only conveyed Giancarlo's love, but, in Italian it, signified a crossing of borders, a sense of being at home in another world, in Giancarlo's world.

Giancarlo melted when Oliver peered at him with his blue orbs - piercing, radiant, innocent, and full of wonder and imagination. Oliver's taut torso pressing against his chest felt reassuring and revitalizing. He could feel his energy rise, his muscles flex, his pulse race, and his heart pound as Oliver slid down, kissing first the outlines of his shoulders, followed by the hollow of his side, and finally the part of his abdomen just inside his hip where a slight turn of his nose would graze his sex, sending it quivering with anticipation.

Oliver savored Giancarlo's scent – earthy, sweet, aromatic, caramel-like. As his skin moistened with arousal, Oliver could taste the subtle changes, sending him into a frenzy as he devoured him with abandon. Giancarlo gave himself up to Oliver's appetite, relishing the passion riding over him.

Even as their bodies hardened in desire, the boundaries of each gave way to a deep and intoxicating union. Oliver sensed swells of pleasure rise within Giancarlo. Each wanted to delay climax, prolonging the heightened sensation of their love. Pressed closely, Oliver could feel the mounting waves of pleasure in Giancarlo's body and felt his own body explode as Giancarlo climaxed under him. They writhed in joy, release, and satisfaction.

Giancarlo placed his hand affectionately on Oliver's buttocks, squeezing the last tremors of pleasure out of his partner. Oliver rested his head on Giancarlo's chest, listening to his heart pound and his chest rise with each breath. They both laid with each other for a protracted period, neither in a hurry to reclaim his autonomy. Eventually, they got up, went to the bathroom, and slipped under the warm duvet covers, holding each other tenderly as snow fell outside the window.

Over the next few days, they got into a pleasant rhythm: a leisure breakfast, a full day on the slopes, a nap, dinner, and a walk into town for an espresso or gelato. Luca picked up skiing quickly and enjoyed spending time with his dads on the snow. Giancarlo and Oliver were encouraged that he liked the sport so much and looked forward to future trips.

On their fourth day of skiing, they took the Dolonne gondola up to Plan Checrouit and then the next gondola up to the top of the mountain. Giancarlo stepped out of the station and walked out with Oliver and Luca into the bright sunshine. He tossed his skis to the ground and stepped into the bindings. Luca was doing the same, having mastered the technique well. Oliver took pictures. Giancarlo's phone pinged. He pulled it out of his jacket pocket and noticed a text from Maria: "Don't get alarmed, but I have been having some cramps this morning."

"Oh my God," Giancarlo said to Oliver, "I think the baby may be coming."

"What do you mean?" Oliver asked in alarm, looking over at Giancarlo's phone.

"Maria's having some cramping." Giancarlo texted her back: "We'll come back immediately."

She texted back: "No. I'm fine. I'll let you know if you need to come back sooner."

"Oliver, I think we need to get back to Milan. I have a feeling things are going to progress quickly."

Luca noticed the alarm on his fathers' faces and creased his forehead.

"*Andiamo*, Luca. Let's ski to the bottom." Giancarlo directed.

They skied down, turned in their rental equipment, and took the Dolonne gondola to the village below. They checked out of the inn and raced back to Milan. In a couple of hours, Oliver dropped Giancarlo and Luca at Maria's house and returned the rental car to the agency. When he arrived at the apartment, Giancarlo greeted him with a bag in hand and said, "We have to get her to the hospital. She's having contractions."

"Already? This is three weeks early."

"I know," Giancarlo said in alarm.

"Can you take Luca? I'll ride with Maria to the hospital in a taxi."

Oliver nodded, taking Luca by the hand, and following Giancarlo and Maria outside.

A few hours later, a physician came into the waiting room of the hospital and approached Giancarlo and Oliver. "You sister just delivered a very healthy boy."

"How is she doing?" Oliver asked as he jumped up and down with excitement.

"She's recovering and doing well."

"And the baby – was it premature? Any problems?" Giancarlo asked with brows furrowed.

"He came early, but he seems to be healthy. We will monitor him for a few days, but there are no noticeable problems. He was just ready to come out!"

Luca smiled.

"When can we see them?"

"I'll ask the nurse and Maria. When she's a little more composed, you can visit her briefly."

About an hour later, a nurse led Giancarlo, Oliver, and Luca into Maria's room. She was propped up on the bed with a little bundle held in her arms. She had pulled her dark brown hair back and had fastened it with a tie. The nurse had draped a blanket over her and tucked several pillows up under her arms. Her face was flush, but she was radiant and smiling. Luca bounced over to the bed and almost jumped up on it.

"*Luca, attenzione!* *Madrina* is tender from the delivery. Treat her and the baby carefully."

Luca stood back, waiting for permission to approach. "You want to see your brother?" Maria asked.

Luca nodded.

"Here he is!" She turned the bundled boy toward Luca and his dads to see.

Oliver began to tear up, and Giancarlo grabbed his sister's hand.

Giancarlo and Oliver looked at each other, nodded, and said, "Gino. *Benvenuto.* Welcome!"

Luca looked at his dads and creased his forehead. He reached up to touch the baby's hand and said, "*Benvenuto, Francesco.*"

Maria looked at Giancarlo and Oliver curiously. They looked at Luca and at each other. "Luca, your brother's name is Gino."

"No, it's Francesco. Right?" he asked the baby as he held his hand.

"He's so cute," Oliver remarked to Maria. "Are you okay?"

She nodded. "I'm a bit sore and tired, but happy. He came so fast."

"He must have been ready to come out," Giancarlo noted. "Since we're here, we can help you this week."

"That would be great. I thought we would be in Rome. I don't have anything ready for Gino at home – such as formula, diapers, and things like that."

"We'll take care of that."

They remained in the room for a while and then headed home, stopping at a local pharmacy to pick up some items for the baby's arrival. They straightened things up and checked what else they might need to get. "We don't have a bed for Gino," Oliver said to Giancarlo.

"We can make a make-shift crib on the bed in our room with some blankets and pillows. One of us can stay in the room while the other and Luca sleep on the sofa in the living room."

"How are we going to get back to Rome with him?" Oliver pressed further.

"We'll figure that out. Maybe we'll have to rent a car. I don't think a train is a good way to travel with a newborn."

Oliver nodded in affirmation.

"When is Francesco coming home?" Luca interjected.

"Gino's coming home in a couple of days. Are you ready for him?"

"His name is Francesco. Why do you keep calling him Gino?" Luca asked, his forehead furrowed in frustration.

"When a baby is born, the parents give him a name. We gave him the name Gino, like we gave you the name Luca."

"But his name is Francesco. That's what his name was," Luca said emphatically.

Giancarlo looked inquisitively at Oliver, who shrugged his shoulders.

Later, when Luca was watching TV, Giancarlo asked Oliver quietly, "What do you think we should do? Luca seems insistent that his brother's name is Francesco. Where do you think that's coming from?"

"I don't know. The other day he was talking to an imaginary friend while playing. Maybe he's just got a wild imagination and has created this Francesco in his head."

"Should we just change the name? I kind of like Francesco. It would be okay with me," Giancarlo suggested.

"Hmm," Oliver murmured. "I like Francesco, too, but I'm not comfortable with Luca calling the shots. We get to name our baby."

"So, what should we do? He said Francesco was his name – as if in past tense," Giancarlo noted. "Do you believe in past lives?"

"Sometimes I wonder about that. I've even wondered about us – about how quickly we connected, as if we had known each other before. What about you?"

"I'm pretty skeptical of the idea, but I guess you never know," Giancarlo mused.

"How would we know?" Oliver inquired further.

"You mean if there is such a thing as past lives?"

"Yeah," Oliver confirmed.

"Short of hypnotizing Luca, we couldn't know for sure. And I'm not comfortable with that," Giancarlo said emphatically.

"If there is such a thing as past lives, and Luca has recognized his brother as someone he knew, I would hate to traumatize him by forcing him to call his brother Gino. And even if there isn't such a thing as past lives, Luca has clearly imagined a Francesco as his brother. Why don't we go with Francesco?" Oliver suggested.

"I'm okay with that," Giancarlo agreed. "I'll tell Maria. She'll be fine with whatever."

Later, they put Luca to bed and retreated to the living room to have a drink.

"What a day, huh?" Oliver began.

Giancarlo looked lost in thought. He murmured, "Hmm, hum."

"Are you okay?"

Giancarlo nodded yes, but he didn't look okay. He tentatively said, "This parenting thing is really something."

"What do you mean?"

"Well, you have this idea in your head of what your family will be like, but you really don't get to choose the personality of your children."

Oliver nodded for him to continue.

"I love Luca. He's cute, bright, affable. But I get nervous that he will be odd."

"How so?" Oliver inquired further.

"His vivid imagination, for one. His premonitions. His odd relationship with the house. And now this crazy narrative about his brother being called Francesco. Maybe he's just a bright, creative child. But what if that's not the case? What if he's imaginative to the point of being out of touch with reality? What if he creates his own world detached from the real one?"

"All kids are quirky at some point and live in their own worlds. That's normal," Oliver tried to reassure him, although he had his own doubts as well.

"When do they grow out of it?" Giancarlo asked.

"I don't know. Maybe when they go to school and socialize more with other kids and study various subjects."

"Back to the idea of past lives," Giancarlo interjected, intrigued by the conversation they had just had. "Do you think there's anything to it?"

Oliver looked off into the distance and then turned back to Giancarlo. "When I first came to Italy to find my biological father, I thought about it some. Why are we who we are? Is it our genes? Is it our upbringing? Or is there something deeper within us – a memory of past lives that we inherit and work through in addition to our current genetic makeup and family? Then, when George took me to see Michelangelo's 'David' in Florence, I was struck with the incredible genius the work represented and wondered – where does all of that talent come from at such an early age?"

Giancarlo nodded and then asked, "So, what do you think?"

"As much as I'm intrigued by it, I'm not sure how it works. We often talk about messages from the departed or communication with them. If they've departed but also reincarnated, how does all of that work?"

"What do you mean?" Giancarlo pressed him further.

"Well, if I wanted to communicate with Henry, my biological father who is dead, I would direct my thoughts to the afterlife, to heaven. And, if I felt like there was a connection with him or a message from him, that would all make sense. But, if there's such a thing as past lives and reincarnation, and if I wanted to connect with him, how would that work? Could one both communicate with the departed in heaven and with their reincarnated self that is somewhere here on earth? Where is Henry? Is he in heaven, is he back on earth, or is he in both places? Is the category of person and place too three dimensional? Might we think about states of being? And could one be in multiple states at the same time so that there's a part of us here, another dimension of ourselves in so-called heaven, and perhaps other elements of ourselves living in various moments of time?"

"That seems bizarre," Giancarlo said, furrowing his brow.

"But I'm sure people had similar opinions when Freud elaborated theories of how the psyche splits between the unconscious, a conscious ego, and a superego. Now it's mainstream. And think about Jung and his theories about the collective unconscious. Maybe there's more to personhood than the ego and unconscious."

As Oliver vocalized his considerations, an eerie thought came over him. What if Luca was Henry reincarnated? What if there was some karmic thing he and his father had to work out, and now he was raising him?

Oliver looked like he had zoned out. Giancarlo nudged him and said, "So, what about Luca? Do you think some of his behavior has to do with a past life?"

"I'm not sure. And to tell you the truth, it frightens me. I can deal with parenting a kid who shares our genetic traits and whose personality is shaped by our family, but I'm unnerved by the idea that our child is someone else who has moved in – an adult in a child's body – someone who has a whole history of relationships and issues and brings them to us. That's really scary!" Oliver added.

Giancarlo's eyes widened with apprehension at Oliver's suggestions. "That's why I am more comfortable with the idea that Luca is just imaginative, creative, and smart."

Oliver nodded, but he couldn't help but wonder whether there was more to Luca than that. "Shall we go to bed?" he asked.

"Yes. I'm exhausted and, if Francesco and Maria come home tomorrow, it's going to be quite a day!"

They put away their glasses and tiptoed into the room they were sharing with Luca. They looked over at his small bed and smiled as they held each other tightly. Giancarlo leaned toward Oliver and gave him a warm kiss. "He'll be fine! He's such a gift."

Oliver rubbed his hands over Giancarlo's shoulder and then took his hand and pulled him toward the bed. They undressed, slipped under the covers, and fell into a deep sleep.

8

Chapter Eight – Aunt Rosa

Oliver stood outside customs at the Rome airport waiting for his moms to exit the opaque doors. Anna texted when they arrived, but 30 minutes had already passed. He assumed they had gotten delayed in lines at passport control. He glanced up from his phone and finally noticed Rita exiting the door and looking for him. Anna was right behind her.

"Mom and ma – over here," he exclaimed, waving them down.

Anna and Rita pulled their suitcases toward him and gave him a big hug. "Oliver, you are a sight for sore eyes! You're getting handsomer every day. It must be something in the Italian water," Anna noted with humor, looking around at the handsome men standing nearby.

"Look at the two of you. I can't believe you're here!"

Anna and Rita were both attorneys at pharmaceutical companies in Boston. Anna was from the Midwest. She had luminous, fair skin and blonde hair. Rita had grown up in an Italian family with roots in the Abruzzi region of Italy. She had dark curly hair, olive complexion, and a mercurial temperament.

They were alarmed when Oliver first went to Rome to meet his biological father six years ago. During his few weeks in Rome, Oliver came out as gay, met Giancarlo, and moved to Rome. At first, they objected to their son's relationship. Giancarlo was ten years older, and the idea that Oliver was moving in with his first significant gay relationship alarmed them. But, over the years, they developed an affection for Giancarlo and were increasingly confident that he and Oliver made a great couple.

"How's Francesco? We can't wait to see him."

"He's fine and a handful. Giancarlo is looking after him and working from home. Luca is with Paola, but she will bring him to our place when I text her."

They made their way to the center of Rome and to the front of Oliver's and Giancarlo's new home. "Here we are," Oliver said to his mothers.

"I like the neighborhood. It seems quieter than Trastevere," Rita noted as she glanced out of the taxi window.

"It is. We like the place. I can't wait for you to see it."

Oliver opened the large wooden doors of the building and guided them through the courtyard. He helped them up the staircase with their luggage and saw Giancarlo waiting just outside the entrance to their unit. "Anna and Rita, welcome!" he said as he gave them kisses on their cheeks.

Luca approached from behind, beaming as he saw his grandmothers. "Grandma Anna and Granny Rita!" he yelled in excitement.

"Luca! How's our prince?"

"I have a new brother. Do you want to come see him?"

They nodded. Luca took hold of Anna's wrist and led them enthusiastically upstairs to the study, which had been made into a make-shift nursery. Giancarlo and Oliver followed. Anna and Rita went inside the room with Luca, who approached Francesco's bed. He held his hand up to his mouth. "Shh. He's asleep."

Anna and Rita chuckled. They peered down into the bed.

Francesco looked like Luca when he was a baby. He had dark hair, round cheeks, and a cute mouth. He must have sensed their presence and stirred, finally opening his eyes. Luca reached his hand toward his brother and Francesco grabbed hold of him, smiling, his dimples appearing on both sides of his mouth.

"Ahh, he's so precious," Anna said, placing her hand gently on her grandson's chest.

Giancarlo reached down and lifted Francesco up. "Do you want to hold him?" he asked Anna and Rita.

"Could we?" Rita said excitedly.

He extended Francesco to her. She took him in her arms. He looked up at her and smiled. Anna poked her finger toward him, and he grabbed for it. "He's adorable," Rita murmured. "Just like Luca," she added, making sure her other grandson got attention, too.

"We're very fortunate," Oliver remarked, placing a hand on Luca's shoulder. "Let's go downstairs. It's time for his feeding, and we can visit better there."

They went back downstairs to the parlor. "Can I get you some coffee, something to eat?" Giancarlo offered, as he went into the kitchen to prepare a bottle.

"Some coffee would be great. I can't drink the stuff on the plane!" Anna replied.

"Me, too," Rita added.

Giancarlo pressed the button on the espresso machine, and it hummed into action, pushing out two *caffè lunghi* for Anna and Rita. "A croissant?" he asked.

Anna nodded. Oliver retrieved the coffees and croissants and brought them into the parlor. Giancarlo fed Francesco. They all sat on the sofa and visited, Luca sitting contently nearby, his legs rocking on the edge of the chair.

"We're so glad you could change your flights and come sooner.

We don't know what we would do without your help," Giancarlo began.

"You can't imagine how excited we are," Anna noted.

"He's a lot of work," Oliver remarked.

"You guys just relax. We can pick up a lot of slack while you get back to your work routines. We can take care of Luca, too."

"He begins preschool next week. He'll be in school for half a day," Oliver remarked.

"We love your new place. It feels like you've been here for longer than a month," Anna said as she looked around the room.

"Well, with our old furniture, it feels like home. But, perhaps more than that, it suits us. We like the feel of the place. We still need to make some renovations, particularly of the study and some adjustments to the kitchen."

"How did you find it?"

"By accident," Giancarlo said and then added, "or maybe not. Luca tripped in front of it on our way to another place we were looking at. We noticed the for-sale sign and, well, here we are." Anna and Rita looked at each other curiously and glanced over at Oliver, who raised his eyebrows, indicating that there was more to the story.

"Mom and ma, are you sure your jobs are okay with you working from here for a couple of weeks?"

"Yes, we cleared it with our respective places," Rita said. "We had been planning to take some vacation anyway, so it's fine."

"Let me take your suitcases up to the bedroom. You can sleep in Luca's new bed. He'll sleep in our room, and the baby in the study," Oliver explained, standing up and grabbing hold of their suitcases. Then he added, "What did you put in these? They weigh a ton!"

"It's winter in Boston and here. You never know what you'll need."

Rita and Anna both stood up to help Oliver. They walked upstairs and into the bedroom. "Francesco is so cute. You must be excited," Anna said.

"We are," Oliver beamed.

"Weren't you going to name him Gino?" Rita asked.

"We were, but Luca kept calling him Francesco. He said that was his name."

"Odd. What do you think that's about?"

"We've been noticing some things lately."

"Like what?"

"He talks with an imaginary friend a lot in a variety of unrecognizable languages. He seems to have a vivid imagination, particularly around weather. Remember, I mentioned that to you on the phone back in the fall? He has premonitions – like he knows when you are about to call. And he seems oddly familiar with the new house."

"That's normal. Kids have their own worlds, and that's good."

"We got concerned and visited with a psychologist last week."

"Everything okay?" Rita said with alarm.

"Yeah. The doctor tested Luca, and he is normal on all counts."

"I detect a hesitation," Rita noted.

"I'm not convinced it is just normal childhood imagination. I think something else is up."

"What does Giancarlo think?" Rita pressed further.

"Well, that's the problem. He's relieved and in agreement with the psychologist – that it's just normal childhood development and creativity. He gets nervous when I raise questions about whether Luca might be gifted in some other sense."

"What do you mean?"

"Well, that perhaps he has special gifts of intuition or even powers." Oliver hesitated and then added, "I know that may sound strange to you."

Rita nodded no and then said, "I never told you this. Remember Aunt Rosa, grandma's sister?"

"You're not going to start again with your Aunt Rosa?" Anna interjected with alarm from the parlor.

"Yes. I think it's relevant," Rita affirmed. "Do you remember her, Oliver?"

He nodded. "You mean the one in Brooklyn?"

"Yes. I think we visited her a few times when you were younger."

"She had that cool house on Park Slope."

"Exactly."

"Well, everyone said she was a witch, *una strega*."

"Wow!"

"Yes, and in those days, it was not a good thing. This was all before *Harry Potter*. People were prejudiced and mean."

"Why did they think she was a witch?"

"She had an uncanny intuition. She could pick up all sorts of things by just shaking someone's hand. Today, people would probably call her an empath or just say she has good intuition. But, in those days, people were afraid of her. But from my vantage, she was one of the most loving people I ever met."

"I remember her fondly, too. She had a room full of toys for us cousins."

"Yes, she encouraged you all to play and to create."

"In retrospect, I now remember a box full of gemstones we used to create colorful designs."

"Yes, she was into using crystals to protect herself and to create good vibes at her house."

"You and ma taught me to trust my vibes, my feelings."

"That was what I learned from Rosa. It's always served me well. Our culture shames intuition and emotions. That's why kids eventually lose the gifts they have when they are younger. Rosa didn't, and it served her well into her old age."

Anna creased her forehead, suggesting she wasn't totally on board.

"So, you don't think we need to worry about Luca?"

"On the contrary. It sounds like he is very gifted. If you can keep him from losing those gifts, he will be a special person and offer a lot to others," Rita suggested.

Oliver looked out of the window and rubbed his chin, pondering what his mother had just shared. He opened some drawers in the armoire and unpacked things from the suitcases. "What else did Aunt Rosa do?"

"I don't remember everything, but I recall she did Tarot readings for neighbors and had a gift for helping people conquer their anxieties. She used to prepare herbal remedies and coach people in setting intentions. I learned a lot just listening in on her sessions."

"Can you observe Luca over the next couple of weeks and let me know what you notice? Don't bring this up with Giancarlo. He's pretty skeptical, and he'll think we are both kooky."

"It's our secret," she said, glancing over at Anna with a sheepish look.

Several days later, Oliver and Giancarlo were at work. Anna was out shopping, and Rita was watching Francesco and Luca. Luca was flipping the pages of a new book Oliver had gotten for him, and Rita was sipping coffee and reading the Boston Globe online.

"Luca, tell me a little more about Francesco," she began, seeing if Luca might be forthcoming.

Luca looked up from his book and smiled. "Well, he's an artist."

"You don't say," she remarked with excitement and curiosity.

"Yes, although he's little now, when he was older, he used to paint."

"And where was that?"

"Here, although we moved later."

"Tell me more," Rita said with nervous excitement.

Luca looked perplexed, as if he were struggling. Rita then said, "Go on, trust your thoughts."

"He didn't like me at first."

"What do you mean?" Rita pressed him.

"Well, I guess I didn't like him, either."

"Why?"

"I don't know. I like him now."

"That's what's important," Rita remarked.

"Your dad says you speak a lot of languages."

Luca nodded.

"More than Italian and English."

Luca nodded again.

"What do you speak?" she asked.

Luca looked perplexed. He didn't seem to know how to answer the question. Rita knew Spanish and asked him, "*Cuando estuviste con Francesco, qué hablaron?*"

A look of recognition overcame Luca's face. He answered, "*El hablaba Italiano.*"

"And you – what did you speak?"

"*Mas.*"

"More?"

Luca nodded.

Rita was surprised by Luca's facility with Spanish and the interesting notions about Francesco. She didn't know where to take the conversation, and worried that perhaps she was in over her head. She let Luca return to his book. She opened her iPad and searched information on the internet about past lives. There was an article about children and their memories. It noted that some kids are born with more awareness of past lives or past relationships. As they grow older, those experiences are invalidated in favor of their current lives, and they lose touch. The article mentioned familiarity with other languages, special talents that carried over from a former life, recognition of relationships from past lives, ailments or physical features they inherit, and fears or concerns that represent unresolved matters. She couldn't wait for Oliver to get home from work so she could discuss the information with him.

Around three in the afternoon, Oliver returned from a tour he was leading. Luca was napping, Anna was working on a project, and Rita was making ravioli in the kitchen. Oliver gave Rita a kiss and made himself a coffee.

"So, how did the day go? Did Luca behave?" Oliver asked as he took a sip of his espresso.

"Yes. We had a good time. We took care of Francesco, read books, and talked."

"What did you talk about?"

Rita raised her eyebrows, looking up from one of the ravioli she was pressing closed. "Well, we had an interesting conversation."

"I'm all ears."

She recounted the conversation they had and concluded, "I think he's definitely tuned into a former life – and his brother was very much a part of it."

"He said Francesco was an artist?" Oliver asked to confirm one of the points Rita had recounted.

She nodded.

"And that they had lived in this house?"

She nodded again and then added, "At times, he seemed at a loss for making sense of things. I'm sure it must be hard if you are living in this life and trying to make sense of another you are remembering or perhaps evening living concurrently."

"That would explain his familiarity with the house," Oliver mused. He rubbed his chin and then continued, "What do you think of the idea of past lives?"

"I was always skeptical, but after what Luca said, I looked things up on the internet. I'm intrigued."

"Me, too. But what about other things such as his intuition, premonitions, and ability to impact weather?"

"Like I said before, Aunt Rosa seemed gifted in those areas, too. She developed her abilities and helped many people."

"I don't want him to be a freak."

"Dear, he won't be. Aunt Rosa wasn't a freak."

"But people thought she was a witch."

"Things are changing. Think of all the kids who have grown up reading *Harry Potter*. Think of how things have changed regarding gay people. It used to be a stigma to be gay. Now people think it's cool to have gay friends. When Aunt Rosa was alive, a lot of people avoided her. Who knows, if she were alive today, people might be more intrigued and drawn to her."

"Maybe you're right, although I'm still uneasy. And Giancarlo is even more reluctant to go there."

"You're both smart and caring men. I'm sure you'll do the right thing for Luca."

"Thanks, mom. You both taught me so much about acceptance and love."

Rita smiled and gave her son a warm hug. "By the way, in the study, I can't seem to get the door to the little closet closed. I had opened it to get some diapers and things, and it won't close."

"I'll check it later." He leaned over the counter and added, "Those ravioli look amazing. What are you stuffing them with?"

"Some are with pumpkin and the others with a veal and bechamel sauce," she said as she pointed to two bowls filled with stuffing. Since her son had moved to Italy, she began to explore her Italian roots, practicing Italian and learning local recipes. She was excited to spend time in their home in the center of Rome.

"Are we having them tonight?"

"Yes – with a nice salad. How does that sound?"

"Wonderful. Let me go upstairs, clean up, and look in on Luca."

Oliver went upstairs and poked his head into the study to make sure Francesco was still asleep. He noticed the door to the closet was ajar, as Rita had mentioned, and went over to close it. It wouldn't close. He bent down and examined the hinges and noticed that at the bottom of the closet there was a tile that had popped loose. He took hold of it and lifted it out of place. He was curious about what was between floors and peered into the space below. The tiles in the closet were all loose, and he lifted them.

Just under the floor, he noticed a few yellowed pieces of paper. He reached down and pulled them up. They were a heavy parchment. He held the first up to the light. The page was full of an old Italian cursive script. He had studied similar documents in his archaeological studies and began to decipher the text. It was difficult to get the gist of things. He wiped the dust off it and continued to peer at the script. The page he was looking at was the continuation of something on a previous sheet.

and ten scudi to the Institute for translations. New books on arrival at Enzo's shop. Meeting on Friday with His Holiness to discuss Fra Luther. 10 – October – 1519. G. Salviati.

"Wow!" Oliver murmured to himself. He reached into the space between the floors and felt more pages. He carefully extracted them and laid them on the floor in front of him. Each page included a date, much like a journal. There were notations about money, appointments, and travel. They were all signed G. Salviati.

Oliver typed G. Salviati into a browser on his phone, and the name Cardinal Giovanni Salviati came up. He was born in 1490 and died in 1553. He was grandson of Lorenzo de' Medici and nephew of Pope Leo X and lived in Rome.

Oliver continued reading the short online biography. Salviati was involved in diplomatic efforts of the papacy in Spain and France. He brought Francesco de' Rossi to Rome to paint frescos in his palace near the Vatican. The artist eventually was known as Francesco Salviati.

At the reference to Francesco Salviati, Oliver's heart skipped a beat. "Oh my God," he said to himself. "I wonder if this is the Francesco Luca is so attached to?"

Oliver ran downstairs to the kitchen with the pages in hand. "Mom, look at these!"

"What honey?" she said, as she saw the look on his face.

"The door wouldn't close upstairs because a tile had popped up. Underneath were a few loose pieces of parchment, probably from a journal. You won't believe this. They are from a Cardinal Salviati."

"Well, that's interesting. Who was he?" she asked, not particularly impressed by the information.

"Get this! Salviati brought an artist from Florence to do work for him. His name was Francesco."

"Ahh," she said, placing the fork she was using to press the ravioli down on the counter, and peering over Oliver's arm onto the pages. "Luca's Francesco, the artist?"

"Yes. It could be. If so, it would appear he might be right about our little Francesco."

"It could just be a coincidence," she noted.

"Ma – Luca said he was an artist, and his name was Francesco. Luca seems familiar with the house – a house where a Francesco lived. Luca must have lived here, too.

"If that's true, who was Luca? Was he the cardinal?"

Oliver rubbed his chin. "Maybe. We'll have to read more of these pages to find out. I'm also wondering if there is a larger book in the walls. Maybe these pages fell out of it."

"Did you do any research on the history of the house when you bought it?"

"We know it has been here since at least the 1400s. So, if the cardinal lived in the 1500s, this could have been his house. However, the online biography says he moved into a palace near the Vatican in 1524. And Francesco, the artist, didn't move to Rome until 1531 or so." Oliver took the pages and laid them on the dining table. They were not numbered, but the dates after each entry allowed him to put them in sequence.

"Look here," he said with excitement to Rita. "There's mention of a Lucia, someone who does translations for him."

"Hmm. Luca, Lucia. That's close, don't you think?"

"Precisely! And you know Luca's ease with languages," Oliver remarked.

"What are you two up to?" Anna asked from a chair in the parlor. You seem awfully excited about something.

"Oh, it's nothing," Rita remarked, knowing Anna didn't buy into past life theories.

"It must be something. Look at the two of you!" she remarked again.

"We found these pieces of parchment under the floor of the study. They appear to be journal entries from a cardinal in the 1500s."

"Hmm," Anna mumbled. "That's fascinating. You'll have to do more research. Sounds like the house has a lot of history." She returned to her work. Rita winked at Oliver.

A while later, Giancarlo arrived. Luca had woken from his nap and was sitting in the parlor watching TV. Oliver was bent over the pieces of parchment. Giancarlo gave his son a kiss, hugged Rita, and approached Oliver from behind, rubbing his shoulders.

"What are you looking at?" he inquired.

"Some floor tile in the study were loose, and I found these pieces of parchment underneath – from the 1500s."

"Wow! Maybe they belong to a previous owner."

"Yes. The previous owner, in this case, was Cardinal Salviati."

"There must have been a lot of clerics that owned buildings in

Rome. It's probably not that remarkable. Who was this Cardinal Salviati?"

"He was a Medici, grandson of Lorenzo de' Medici and nephew of Pope Leo X."

Giancarlo raised his brows. "That is a while back and impressive."

"And he brought a Florentine artist to Rome in 1531. The artist's name was Francesco," Oliver said quietly so that Luca wouldn't hear.

Giancarlo chuckled and said, "Ahh, so you and Rita have concocted a narrative that links Luca's naming his brother Francesco with this Cardinal Salviati?"

Oliver and Rita looked at each other and put their fingers up to their lips. "Shhh." Anna looked up from her chair. Then Oliver said in a low voice, "Luca mentioned to Rita that Francesco was an artist."

"Our Francesco?" Giancarlo asked, his forehead creased.

"Yes. Our Francesco."

"Hmm," he mused to himself. "You know I don't buy into that stuff."

"Well, how do you explain the connections?" Oliver pressed further.

"I'm not sure. Maybe it's just that Luca is picking up on the history of the house. It has a rich history. Maybe past inhabitants left their energy here and there. You know he's got an active imagination. He's just picking up things and then creating interesting stories."

"So, you're more comfortable with the idea of ghosts than past lives?" Oliver asked, again in a whisper.

"I didn't say ghosts. I said he's picking up energy in the house, vestiges of things that happened here."

"How is that any more credible?" Rita asked. "Whether it's ghosts, past lives, or energetic traces, it all involves something beyond the physical and something that transcends ordinary time."

"I'm not averse to things non-material, but I'm not sure the notion of past-lives makes sense," Giancarlo continued. "I've heard too many of my friends talk about being some king or princess or noble in a past life. No one was just an ordinary person."

"I was never inclined to embrace the notion of past lives either," Oliver noted. "But Luca's behavior makes more sense if you do."

"Well, you will have to produce more evidence to convince me," Giancarlo noted.

Rita looked at Oliver and raised her eyebrows. Oliver looked over at Anna, wondering what she thought. "Don't look at me," she noted.

"Maybe the journal entries will say more. What would you say if Luca mentions things in the journal – things that he could only know if he had lived here at that time?" Oliver inquired.

"Then I might have to accept the idea but, until then, I think we have a very imaginative young man who may be picking up on things." He glanced across the room at his son, who was engrossed in a TV show.

Rita looked at Oliver and raised her eyebrow. Then she said, "On another note, who's ready for dinner?"

Anna said, "I am. I'm starved!"

"Let me get some wine?" Giancarlo said, reaching up in a cabinet for a bottle of wine and then in another for some glasses. "Luca," he shouted over the sound of the TV. "Are you ready for dinner?"

Luca nodded, turned off the TV, and walked toward the kitchen. Rita handed him a glass of juice and said, "Why don't you take your seat?"

"I'll get Francesco," Oliver remarked, clearing the sheets of parchment from the table, placing them in a file, and heading upstairs.

Rita boiled the water, dropped the ravioli inside the pot, and mixed the salad. In a few minutes, she drained the ravioli and placed them back in the pan, stirring them with some melted butter and parmesan cheese. She emptied the pan onto a platter and placed it in the center of the table next to the salad.

Oliver returned with Francesco in hand, and Giancarlo handed him a freshly warmed bottle of milk. They all sat at the table and began to eat. Oliver looked over at Luca, who was stabbing one of the pumpkin ravioli with his fork. Luca looked up and smiled. Oliver felt a strange sensation, as if in Luca's glance someone other than his son was gazing at him.

9

Chapter Nine – The Cardinal's Journal

A few months later, Rita and Anna had returned to Boston. Luca spent half-days at pre-school. Oliver watched Francesco when he didn't have tours booked and left him with Paola on other days. Giancarlo continued his work at the bank, attracting more and more wealthy gay clients to a historically conservative institution.

An architect was engaged to do some renovations and updates to the new home, including an extensive overhaul of the study. In the process of demolition, workers found a journal wedged between supports. It had apparently fallen from a higher place and landed on a crossbeam, shaking a few pages loose – the ones Oliver had found under the floor tile.

Oliver spent every free moment deciphering the entries. The journal was from Cardinal Salviati's early years in Rome. From what Oliver could piece together, the cardinal patronized an institute dedicated to the care of orphaned or abandoned women. They were, for the most part, illegitimate daughters of nobles and clerics. In the course of his work, the cardinal discovered that one of the residents was Jewish. Her name was Luz, but the nuns called her Lucia. Her parents had died of the plague. They were refugees from Spain, having come to Rome in the late 1400s. Lucia's father worked in the Vatican library as an archivist and translator. He was an important contributor to work on ancient philosophical manuscripts preserved in Arabic.

After her parents' deaths, Bishop Gian Pietro Carafa, a much-loathed conservative reformer, framed Lucia for a crime. Carafa claimed Lucia was a thief and a witch, accusing her of stealing a grimoire from the Vatican Library. He had her placed in the Institute under house-arrest. Lucia claimed the book was a family heirloom bequeathed by her father. Cardinal Salviati discovered Lucia knew many languages, and he paid the head of the Institute, Madre, a stipend for Lucia's translation work. The cardinal found Lucia to be a brilliant woman and hardly a witch.

The journal entries ended abruptly. Oliver discovered through additional research that Cardinal Salviati bought the Palazzo della Rovere near the Vatican in 1524. It was in Salviati's new home that he brought Francesco de' Rossi to Rome to paint frescos. Francesco eventually came to be known as Francesco Salviati. Oliver was intrigued that an artist would take his patron's name and wondered if there hadn't been some kind of romantic relationship between them.

Palazzo della Rovere ended up in the hands of the Knights of the Holy Sepulchre. In recent years, they leased it out as a hotel, The Columbus. Oliver made several inquiries of the Knights to see if there might not be some manuscripts belonging to the cardinal that were in their possession.

Later that day, Giancarlo returned home from work. Oliver was feeding Francesco, and Luca was drawing in a sketchbook. "Hey guys," he said as he walked in the door. He approached Luca and gave him a hug and kiss. He then leaned over and gave Oliver a kiss.

Oliver wiped Francesco's mouth, burped him, and then took him upstairs to sleep.

"What's for dinner?" Giancarlo inquired as Oliver came back downstairs.

"Can we order pizza? I didn't prepare anything."

"Sure. What do you want on it? I'll call Angelo's place."

"A margherita is good – perhaps with some mushrooms and sausage.

Giancarlo phoned the pizzeria, placed the order, and then opened a bottle of wine. "Any luck with the Knights?" he asked Oliver.

"No. They continue to ignore me. I must be *persona non grata* around here."

"They must not be happy with the symposiums you run in favor of LGBTQ people. Is there someone else who could make a request on your behalf, someone who may have less of a public profile?"

"They'd sniff me out, anyway. It's not like people are clamoring to do research on Cardinal Salviati."

"What about Fr. Flanagan? Maybe he has someone he could send over with connections to the Vatican library."

"That's a great idea," Oliver said, rubbing his chin.

He made inquiries with Fr. Flanagan and a few weeks later, he called Oliver. "Oliver, my colleague gained access to the Knights' archives. He claimed to be doing research on the Medici popes and mentioned that Cardinal Salviati had been a contender for several elections. He hoped to find some journals from his time in Rome."

"Ingenious!" Oliver exclaimed.

"Well, sure enough, he found a journal. It is from Salviati's years at Palazzo della Rovere. They allowed him to take it out of the archives on the condition that it would be safeguarded in the Vatican Library."

"Wow. Is it possible for me to see it?"

"That's why I'm calling. You have a brief window of a month to study it, and then it must be returned. What's your schedule like for the next month?"

"I have a few tours, but I'm not swamped. This will be perfect. How do I gain access?"

"I have already arranged a VIP pass for you through our office. When is the next day you are free? I can meet you and orient you to the library."

"What does the day after tomorrow look like for you?"

"That's fine. Do you want to meet at 9 at Porta Sant'Anna?" Flanagan inquired.

"Perfect. *Ci vediamo lì.*"

Two days later, Oliver made his way to the gate where visitors entered the Vatican City. The first time he had passed through the gate was when his biological father, Henry, had given him a private tour of the Vatican Museums and introduced him to the Pope. Fr. Flanagan had worked with Henry. Oliver discovered that Fr. Flanagan was a secret progressive in the Congregation for Education and, after Henry's death, was instrumental in Oliver's work to advance LGBTQ issues in the Church.

Fr. Flanagan waved from inside the gate. Oliver approached, nodded at the Vatican police inside the office, and walked past the Swiss Guard standing at attention. "Thank you so much for doing this," Oliver said excitedly, shaking Fr. Flanagan's hand.

"It's my pleasure. Why is this journal so important?"

"As I shared with you, when we were doing renovations, we discovered Cardinal Salviati's journal from his first years in Rome. We were intrigued by the story and wanted to find out more."

"Ahh," Fr. Flanagan said, not finding the story all that compelling. Oliver concealed his actual interest. He was more and more convinced that his sons were connected to Francesco, Salviati's resident artist, and Lucia, Salviati's in-house scholar.

Fr. Flanagan led Oliver to the Vatican Library and introduced him to the director. The director was very cordial and led Oliver further into the archives to a desk where the journal was being temporarily kept on loan in a special box.

"I'm impressed that you could get the Knights to release this," the director said to Fr. Flanagan. "They are not usually so gracious."

Flanagan winked at the director who had seen enough in Rome to know that it was wise not to dig too deeply into matters. He explained procedures to Oliver, who expressed his gratitude. Once the director and Fr. Flanagan left, he began reading the journal.

Unlike the earlier journal Oliver found in his home, one that included ledgers for expenses and notations for appointments, this was more of a memoir, a series of reflections. Entries were chronological. He imagined Salviati's secretary must have kept track of household expenses and his appointments in a separate book. The journal seems to have begun just after the sack of Rome in 1527, perhaps an earlier one having been destroyed.

Salviati lamented the pillage Emperor Charles V unleashed on Rome. Salviati was lucky to have escaped to the security of Castel Sant'Angelo, but his staff didn't. The women were raped, and the men were injured as they tried to defend the building from troops. Lucia saved Salviati's library by hiding books in secret cavities throughout the palace. She hid in a closet until the troops left.

Besides restoring order to Rome, the Pope faced challenges in the north with the defection of so many Christians to the reformers – Luther, Calvin and others. Salviati was sympathetic with their call for reform, and he wished the Pope would launch more reforms to preempt their challenges.

As a lover of books, Salviati was intrigued by the printing press. On the one hand, it made learning more accessible to the masses. But the dissemination of knowledge challenged traditional authority, most notably the Church. Instead of reasserting raw power,

Salviati thought priests should be better educated so they could debate intellectually with their parishioners.

Oliver pondered the idea that the world was still dealing with authoritarian religious systems, more concerned about preserving power than embracing reason and scholarship. He imagined how world-altering it must have been to think of a heliocentric world, to ponder the idea of an infinite universe, to hear stories of new continents with indigenous civilizations quite different from European ones.

Oliver recognized the parallels between Salviati's world and his own. The contemporary shift of world views had more to do with the environment and sexuality. The world faced unprecedented environmental challenges requiring a whole new way of collaborating across national boundaries. Changing information about sexuality, gender, and families was transforming society. The heterosexual, patriarchal, and reproductive focus of sexuality was giving way to sexual diversity, changing gender identity, changing gender roles, recognition that love is the foundation of marriage, and the dismantling of patriarchy. This was no less disruptive than Copernicus's observations in Salviati's time or Galileo's a century later.

A section of Salviati's journal caught Oliver by surprise. He noted that Enzo, a book dealer, had obtained a lot of new manuscripts after the sack of Rome in 1527. Looters wanted fortune and nobility needed cash. Salviati was on the lookout for a book Lucia said Bishop Carafa had confiscated from her. He claimed she stole it from the Vatican library. She said it was a gift from her father.

Enzo sent Salviati a message. He had a book from Andalusia, one written in Hebrew, Arabic, and Castilian. Salviati bought it and presented it to Lucia, who was ecstatic. She showed a dedication in the back of the book from her grandmother. Salviati raised his eyes as he thumbed through the book, noticing many curious symbols.

He asked her directly if it was a grimoire, a book of magic. She said it wasn't, but he wasn't convinced.

He and Lucia continued to study Ibn Al'Arabi, a prolific Sufi mystic and philosopher. Salviati felt like his notion that the world is the imagination of God did a better job of dealing with the God-world problem. But he was alarmed when Lucia proposed that human beings, created in image and likeness of God, share in God's ability to imagine worlds into being. Salviati knew this was like Ficino's ideas and others found in the *Hermeticum*. Even though his family (the Medicis) and the Pope supported the revival of Greek humanism, if word got out that he was harboring a sorcerer in his household, his prospects of being elected pope would be doomed.

Oliver was intrigued by the relationship between Francesco de' Rossi and Cardinal Salviati. He skimmed the journal to see if he could find mention of Francesco. Andrea del Sarto recommended an artist – Francesco de' Rossi – to decorate and repair the vaulted ceilings. Salviati was instantly drawn to Francesco. He notes how handsome he was. He was only 21. He was tall and broad shouldered. He had a dark complexion and thick, black hair. He had a prominent forehead and penetrating dark brown eyes.

He thought he was quiet, sullen, and ponderous. He assumed artists needed solitude and could become irritable if their work wasn't flowing as they wanted. Salviati found Francesco intimidating and alluring at the same time.

As he read further, Oliver discovered antipathy between Lucia and Francesco, much to Salviati's chagrin. He was proud to have a resident artist and scholar, but he seemed oblivious to how they vied for his attention.

Oliver tired as he struggled to decipher the old Italian script. He took copious notes. He glanced at his watch and realized if he left now, he could stop by the Columbus Hotel – the former Palazzo della Rovere (Salviati's palace) – before heading to Paola's to pick up Luca.

Salviati's former residence was on the Via Conciliazione, a grand boulevard constructed during the time of Mussolini to celebrate the Concordat with the Vatican. Much of the old medieval neighborhood was destroyed to create magnificent views of St. Peter's, but some of the more substantial buildings, including Salviati's, were preserved.

Oliver meandered from the Porta Sant' Anna toward the massive St. Peter's Square. Tourists and pilgrims were lining up to enter the great basilica. Late afternoon sunshine illuminated the twin fountains, spraying water on the dark cobblestone pavement. Oliver glanced up at the façade of St. Peter's and the ribbed dome designed by Michelangelo gleaming in the light.

When he first came to Rome six years ago, he used to stand in front of the church with mouth agape and tears streaking down his cheeks. The dimensions of the building and the history it represented were overwhelming. He chuckled as he recalled accompanying his biological father, Henry, through the excavations under the structure. The old Roman mausoleums marked the perimeter of a small plot used by Christians and Christian sympathizers to bury St. Peter after his death in the nearby circus. That tour helped solidify his interest in becoming an archaeologist.

As he walked through the square, he felt less and less like an observer and more and more a participant, someone who had become part of the fabric of the city and was involved in shaping its future. He turned down the Via Conciliazione and walked up to Salviati's palace. He sat on a marble bench in front of the grand residence and looked up at the impressive wooden eves hanging over the rust-orange stucco façade. Several tourists walked through the old doorway leading into a large, sunny courtyard.

He sat quietly in front of the building. Salviati's journal entries drifted through his mind. It seemed surreal that he and Giancarlo owned Salviati's first home and that their family seemed so connected to Salviati's household. He thought about a building like the Palazzo della Rovere – a structure made of wood, stone, plaster, and clay. It had witnessed countless souls passing through – people making it their home, nurturing relationships, forging alliances, advancing causes, and then moving on. The building didn't change.

With a sense of foreboding and uncertainly, he pondered the question of whether his sons – Luca and Francesco – had lived here in another age. He was struck by the defiant permanence of the structure in the face of the comings and goings of generations. But as he thought about his sons and their connection to the residence, he wondered what was permanent and what was transitory. Was the building like a hologram, something that appeared real and substantial but through which more enduring realities – the persons who inhabited it – continued to appear from age to age? The stories people lived and the challenges they sought to work through seemed to repeat themselves. What was real and what was imagined or projected? Might it be that the world is the unfolding of imagination, a place where consciousness takes form, lives, creates, and loves?

Oliver glanced back at the dome of St. Peter's. Over the centuries, the Vatican hill had stood at the crossroads of so much change. In the 1st century, Rome sought to assert its power over a small religious movement only to be overwhelmed by the burgeoning faith three hundred years later when Constantine erected a massive basilica over St. Peter's tomb. In the 1500s, the ground had shifted again. Whole new continents, peoples, and religions were discovered, a Reformation challenged Rome's hegemony on spirituality and views on sexuality, the Ottoman Empire threatened Europe, and the printing press democratized knowledge. Michelangelo's dome sought to recenter the world around Rome, to forge a new paradigm of authority and power.

Oliver wondered if the current age was simply a re-staging of the same challenges Rome faced in the 1500s. The discovery of vast regions of outer space was decentering the universe. The internet was making almost all the information known to humankind available in a few clicks. Profound changes were occurring around gender, sexuality, and family types. And new paradigms of spirituality were emerging as quantum physics suggested that consciousness shapes matter and that we all are connected in a time-space continuum.

Did certain individuals in the 1500s suffer a loss of nerve, unable to take the steps that would have forged a new cultural and religious paradigm? Were they blinded by their own biases or gripped by vested interests in perpetuating old models of power, spirituality, and gender? Most importantly, were he and his sons pivotal in one age – for better or for worse - and now being given an opportunity to make further strides in the current age?

Later that evening, after dinner, Oliver shared some preliminary information with Giancarlo. "I'm just getting started, but it would appear that Lucia and Francesco were part of the Cardinal's household. Francesco was an artist engaged to paint ceilings in his palazzo, and Lucia was organizing much of the Cardinal's growing library. She made several translations for him."

"*Una coincidenza*, I continue to maintain," Giancarlo said.

"Get this, though. In several entries, the Cardinal laments the hostility between Lucia and Francesco."

"So?"

"My mom mentioned that Luca said he and Francesco didn't like each other, but now they do."

"You'll have to have more evidence than that to convince me that our kids are the reincarnation of two people from the 16th century."

"Well, here's the *pièce de résistance*! Cardinal Salviati mentions that he thinks Lucia may be a sorcerer."

"A what?"

"*Una strega.*"

Giancarlo's eyes widened. "What did she do?"

"I haven't gotten that far yet. The library closed, and I had to leave. I'll do more reading later in the week. But if there is a connection between our boys and Francesco and Lucia, then Luca's abilities – or whatever you want to call them – might make more sense."

"I'm still not buying it. I think Luca simply has a wild imagination and is very intuitive."

"Maybe so. But maybe that's what magic or *stregoneria* is – intuition and imagination."

"What do you mean?"

"Have you ever wanted something really bad, and you put your mind to it? Isn't that about setting the intention, imagining what you want?"

"But then you do things to make it happen."

"Yes, but often things happen not so much because we put things in place but because we really desired or imagined them. Sometimes things happen even despite what had been set in place. Luca has a powerful imagination, and interesting things happen. Isn't that a way of talking about power – the power to influence the outcome of things?"

"Okay – the power of positive thinking, right?"

"Yes. And why isn't that magic?"

Giancarlo was stumped. He realized that positive thinking implied buying into the notion that reality could be influenced not just by material cause and effect, but by imagination as well. And he recalled a few lectures in physics from his years at the university that talked about the double-slit experiment, where quanta or photons were shaped by the act of observation. Reality seemed to be changed by consciousness.

"Think about Luca's waving the clouds away at San Felice Circeo. Through his own imagination, weather changed. And it didn't happen just once. Just the other day he wanted to go outside, and it was raining. I saw him stand at the window and stare. In a short while, the rain stopped, and the sky brightened."

"*Ancora, una coincidenza.*"

"But a lot of coincidences add up. Eventually, one has to recognize that something is going on."

"We'll see. Right now, I want to snuggle up next to you in bed. Are you feeling the force as I imagine that?"

"I'm getting hard. Does that count?"

Giancarlo looked down at Oliver's crotch and realized he was aroused. For a moment he relaxed his guard and thought to himself – maybe there is something to be said about mind over matter. He grabbed Oliver's hand and led him upstairs. They poked their head in Luca's and Francesco's room – both were asleep. They walked quietly to their room and toward the bed.

Giancarlo reached around the back of Oliver's head and pulled him close, giving him a kiss. "I never get enough of this," he said, as he rubbed his hands over Oliver's shoulders and squeezed his firm biceps.

Oliver began to unbutton Giancarlo's shirt, sliding his hands up under the fabric and massaging his pecs that were getting firm. "I still remember when you first cast your spell on me."

"Ah, yes. You mean the evening you pretended you weren't gay?"

Oliver grinned, recalling the sexual confusion he felt when he was 20 and the sudden illumination he had when he met Giancarlo.

Giancarlo pulled Oliver down next to him on the bed. When they first met six and a half years earlier, Giancarlo was instantly drawn to Oliver's exotic surfer look – his shiny blonde hair, blue eyes, dimples, and dark complexion. He had an enchanting innocence to him, curious and eager to embrace new adventures.

Oliver traced his fingers over Giancarlo's brows – luscious, dark, and alluring. He gazed into his eyes and felt Giancarlo's warm breath hovering over his mouth as their lips grazed each other and then joined.

Giancarlo leaned his head back and looked up at Oliver, scrutinizing his face for the dimples that always presaged a playful exchange. "*Ecco*," he murmured as they appeared, Oliver pulling back Giancarlo's collar and kissing his neck.

Giancarlo rubbed his hands over Oliver's shoulder and pulled him close. Although Giancarlo was older and Oliver looked up to him as someone with more experience, wisdom, and perspective, it was Giancarlo who longed for the security and innate wisdom that always flowed from his companion – an unassuming emotional intelligence far more advanced than Oliver's chronological years.

Oliver kept drifting off to the world of Salviati, Francesco, and Lucia. Each time he closed his eyes and traveled to that other world, he felt the firm, aroused body of Giancarlo drawing him back to the present. He felt Giancarlo's soft hands take hold of his sex. He arched his back and moaned as he felt the long, warm strokes bring him to the brink. He could feel Giancarlo's hardness searching for the folds of his body. They both gave themselves over to each other, an acceleration of touch, a pounding of their hearts, and an intense craving for release and union.

They collapsed in each other's embrace. They woke an hour later, realizing they had fallen asleep. Both finished undressing and slipped under the covers, falling back into a sound and peaceful sleep.

10

Chapter Ten – The Cardinal's Love

Two days later, Oliver returned to the Vatican library for a full day of research. Luca was at pre-school, and Francesco was with Paola, who would pick Luca up later. He settled into his seat and opened Salviati's journal. He skimmed to a section that referenced Francesco's work on the ceiling of the palace. He chuckled as he saw not-so-subtle references to Francesco's physique as the hot summer days settled in. Francesco would eventually remove his sweaty shirt and work bare-chested. Although Marta and Stefano brought him refreshments, Salviati wrote that he enjoyed bringing in cool lemonade to Francesco to see how his work was progressing. There were more and more references to Francesco, to his work, to their conversations in the courtyard, and to Salviati's satisfaction with their friendship.

In the middle of a passage, Oliver's phone pinged. Giancarlo texted him: "Oliver, there's a problem at Luca's school. I'm heading to the school, now. Can you meet me there?"

Oliver called him. "Giancarlo, what's the problem?"

"Luca's teacher called me. They pulled him out of the class."

"Why?"

"He was getting belligerent."

"That's not like him. Did the secretary say why?"

"No. She wants to talk with us in person."

A little while later, Oliver walked into the office of the preschool and met Giancarlo, who was holding Luca's hand.

"Luca, what's the matter?"

"Martino and Lorenzo were making fun of me. We were drawing pictures of our families, and I drew you and papa. They laughed and said I was *strano* for having two dads. They didn't want to sit at my table."

Oliver gave his son a big hug and said, "*Ti voglio bene.* You're not strange. You are a wonderful and beautiful person."

Giancarlo looked at his son and said, "What happened next?"

"Martino and Lorenzo started yelling, *frocio.* What does that mean?"

"It's a bad word for someone who loves someone of the same sex – like papa and I," Oliver said.

"Then all the other kids began yelling *frocio, frocio, frocio.*"

Giancarlo stared at Oliver, who started walking toward the school office. "Oliver," Giancarlo said, taking a hold of his arm, "I already spoke to Maestra Castello, and she says there's nothing she can do. Parents don't want their kids associating with someone like Luca who has two gay dads."

"That's outrageous," Oliver said in reply, giving Luca another forceful hug. He asked Luca, "How are you doing?"

Luca nodded without saying anything. He seemed emotional, fighting back tears. He said timidly, "Martino's chair fell backwards," then he grinned.

"What?" Giancarlo inquired.

"When the kids were yelling *frocio, frocio, frocio,* I saw Martino fall backwards."

"And what about Lorenzo?" Oliver asked as he glanced at Giancarlo, wondering if he had the same suspicion. Did Luca imagine Martino falling and, in some way, cause it?

"Lorenzo got frightened when Martino fell. He stopped yelling until the other students joined. Then he started coughing."

"Hm," Oliver murmured to himself. "So, what are we going to do?" he asked Giancarlo.

"I'm not sure what we can do. If we challenge things, people could raise questions about my role at the bank or make life more difficult for Luca."

"Are there any other schools we could send him to that are more progressive, who have a more inclusive policy?" Oliver asked.

"We can look. In the meantime, we can have him stay with Paola in the mornings."

"I don't want to walk away from this."

Giancarlo nodded unconvincingly. They held Luca's hands and walked home.

Later, after Francesco and Luca had gone to bed, Oliver and Giancarlo sat on the sofa, each with a generous brandy in hand, and chatted.

"The more I think about it, the more determined I am to bring Luca back to the school. If we can talk with him and help him feel comfortable, it will be a big step forward for him and for us," Oliver stated.

"Why should he bear the burden of society's prejudices?" Giancarlo pleaded.

"We all do. But I don't want Luca to internalize the shame society wants to project on him. You know what that is like. Why should he have to carry this around all his life? We can give him the tools he needs to feel pride in who his family is."

Giancarlo shook his head. Oliver could tell he was worried about how this might impact his work at the bank and said, "Maybe this is a wake-up call for all of us. It's an opportunity to embrace our dignity and trust in the goodness of others."

"I don't know," Giancarlo said, continuing to shake his head. "I'll ask around and see if there is a more welcoming school."

"That's fine, but if there isn't, we need to face this head on."

Giancarlo just stared.

A week later, Oliver dropped Francesco off at Paola's house. He walked Luca to a new school they found. Oliver returned to the Vatican library and continued reading Salviati's journal.

Oliver always wondered why Francesco de' Rossi took Salviati's name. He assumed there must have been some kind of romantic relationship between them, but he had never seen any evidence documenting it until he opened the journal and an extensive passage jumped out at him.

Salviati described a reception for Francesco and the unveiling of the vaulted ceiling. He noted that Francesco had already been given three commissions from other households. He remarked how handsome he had become as he matured. People kept referring to him as 'Salviati's artist.' He was, at first, alarmed, but then he grew more comfortable with the idea.

Later, Salviati describes a conversation with Francesco. Francesco relates that some people believe they are lovers. Salviati is alarmed and rejects the idea. Francesco discloses that he finds Salviati very attractive and treasures their relationship. Oliver thought Salviati was curiously defensive in the journal – exaggerating his shock and surprise at Francesco's declaration, particularly after earlier physical descriptions Salviati had made of Francesco in the journal. He went to great lengths to accept Francesco's friendship, but rejected anything more.

Oliver wasn't convinced Salviati was as innocent as he described. Another set of entries described the political situation of Rome. Salviati was alarmed that Bishop Gian Pietro Carafa had started a moral purge and had begun to harass clerics and their households. Carafa sought to reform the clergy, and he was in the process of revealing all sorts of sexual liaisons and indiscretions amongst the clergy. Salviati was not unsympathetic with the cause, but he thought Carafa went too far and was perhaps attempting to conceal or deflect attention from his own proclivities.

Oliver took a break for lunch, walking to the nearby Borgo Pio for a plate of pasta and some wine. The neighborhood held troubling memories for him. It was here that he had confronted his biological father, Henry, for his decision to remove gay teachers from Catholic schools. After Henry's death, it was in this same neighborhood that he learned more of Henry's self-loathing and the tortuous struggle to keep his own desires at bay. Oliver had gradually grown to appreciate how the desire for institutional advancement could lead someone to deny their own identity and project self-hatred onto others. He felt anger and sympathy for his father and realized what a toll Henry's strategy had taken on his own health, leading to a crushing and painful cancer.

He was deep in thought when the waiter approached and asked him if he needed anything. "*No, grazie. Sto bene così.*"

But as he said those words, he realized he wasn't okay. The memories had stirred something – an unsettledness, restlessness, and dread. It was almost as if he could feel the battle raging inside his father and linked them with Salviati's reflections. "Salviati was going through the same struggle," he murmured to himself.

He quickly finished his lunch, paid the bill, and raced back to the library. He scoured the journal for more references to Francesco. As he moved forward in the journal, fewer notes were made about Lucia and philosophy and more about Francesco and his art. The dates roughly corresponded to Salviati at the age of fifty. Oliver realized Francesco would have been roughly thirty years old.

Oliver continued to read further in Salviati's journal. There were extensive reflections on the effort of Pope Paul III to counter the reformation in northern Europe. There were calls for a council. The pope confirmed the founding of several new religious orders, prominent among them, the Society of Jesus – the Jesuits.

Salviati seemed alarmed that Gianpietro Carafa was close to getting approval from Pope Paul III to form an inquisition in Rome. The inquisition in Spain had wreaked havoc on the lives of many, being used as a weapon to extract money and stoke fear. Salviati was already nervous that Carafa would come after him given his own affiliation with the Medicis and their liberal support of the arts and scholarship.

Oliver was surprised to find a rather transparent entry a few months after the reception honoring Francesco. Oliver chuckled as he read Salviati's words. He was upset that Francesco was returning to Florence. Apparently, someone for whom Francesco was doing a commission had been charged by Carafa for sodomy. Salviati was upset with Francesco's apparent comfort with the relationship the noble had with a friend – both of them widowers. Francesco was afraid Carafa would come after him by association. Salviati assured him he would handle Carafa, but Francesco wasn't convinced. He returned to the safety of his home in Florence.

Oliver noticed a curious side reference in Salviati's notes. Besides Francesco's fear that by association he would be picked up by Carafa, he complained of digestion problems. He thought Lucia was practicing *stregoneria*. He thought she was trying to get rid of him so that she would have unfettered access to and affection from the Cardinal.

Oliver thumbed through the journal and noticed the absence of any further reflections on Francesco until the end, when he asked that funds be sent to Florence for his maintenance. Notable were entries regarding the election of Pope Julius III. Salviati couldn't hide his own disappointment at having been passed over for the papacy. He lamented having tried to appease Carafa and his faction, only then to lose support from more progressive elements. He realized that while hard line reform efforts were gaining traction, people feared a purging of the clergy that would only legitimize Luther's observations and rhetoric. Salviati believed he represented a more moderate and thoughtful approach.

Oliver couldn't help but note parallels between his biological father, Henry, and Salviati. They both seemed tormented by their own proclivities and determined to put on a façade of respectability to advance their careers. Both of their lives ended with disappointment – unrealized aspirations for leadership and lives lived in denial of their affections. How sad, Oliver thought to himself.

A text from Giancarlo stirred Oliver from his pensiveness. "When are you going to be home? I can get dinner ready."

Oliver texted back: "Soon. I'm almost finished. I'll be there at 6:30."

Oliver jotted down a few more notes, closed the journal, and made his way out of the library to the Borgo area. He caught one of the city buses that made a stop near their home. He stopped at the local grocer, picked up a fresh loaf of bread for breakfast, and continued home.

He walked inside and made his way through the parlor to the kitchen. Giancarlo and Luca were preparing dinner, and Francesco was crawling on the floor. His heart pounded as he saw Giancarlo. He was still incredibly sexy, perhaps even more so wearing an apron and stirring sauce on the stove. They kissed, and Luca gave Oliver a big hug.

"How's everyone doing?"

"We're glad you're back. I need some help. Can you change Francesco and then get him ready for dinner?"

"Certainly," Oliver replied. He grabbed Francesco, sniffed his diapers, and said, "Yep, you need a change!"

He brought him upstairs, changed him, and then returned, setting him in his highchair and setting out some baby food he and Giancarlo had prepared earlier in the week. "You ready for dinner, Luca?" he asked.

Luca nodded and climbed into his chair. "How was school?" Oliver asked further.

"I like it better than the other one. Maestra Carafiello is nice."

"What did you do today in class?"

"We learned the alphabet, and we read a book."

"What was the book?"

"It was about two fish who become friends."

Oliver looked at Giancarlo. They both raised their eyebrows.

Oliver asked, "What happens to the fish?"

"One of them helps the other avoid getting eaten by a bigger fish."

"Wow! How did he do that?" Giancarlo inquired.

"He distracted the big fish until his friend could hide," Luca said proudly.

"Why did you like the story?" Giancarlo inquired further.

"Well, the two fish are different – one is orange, and the other is striped," Luca recounted.

"Why do you like that?" Oliver pressed his son.

"We have to learn to like people who are different," Luca said emphatically.

Oliver nodded. "Yes. Why is that important?"

"So, no one feels bad about who they are."

Oliver beamed at Giancarlo, relieved that they had found a school suitable for Luca, one that sought to teach the value of acceptance and inclusion and diversity in a society that was so homogenous. They hoped Luca would grow up without prejudices and feel good about himself.

Giancarlo placed a platter of pasta with meat sauce on the table.

He pulled a salad out of the refrigerator and set it on the table as well. Oliver spooned some pasta onto Luca's plate and then helped himself. "This smells wonderful. I love how you add mushrooms to your sauce. Is that something you picked up somewhere?"

"It was one of my grandmother's secret touches. It's remained part of our family recipe."

"Any new insights into Cardinal Salviati?"

"Well, I'm glad you asked."

Giancarlo creased his forehead, bracing himself for another excursion into the secrets of Renaissance Rome.

"There are a lot of entries that reveal the cardinal's affections for Francesco and less and less mention of Lucia."

"Go on," Giancarlo said as he took another forkful of pasta.

"Salviati was a favorite several times for the papacy, and he seemed to try to court favor with opposing factions – to cover both bases. He mentions his efforts to appease Carafa and his conservative faction, as well as with the more progressive Medici supporters."

"But I gather he was never made pope, right?"

"Right. He kept getting passed over. In fact, just after he died, Carafa was elected pope. He was Pope Paul IV, a much-hated figure in Rome. He created the Jewish ghetto and began a brutal persecution of Jews, homosexuals, and women thought to be witches."

Giancarlo set his fork down and took a long sip of wine, now intrigued by what Oliver was recounting.

"What about he and the artist?"

"It would appear the artist returned temporarily to Florence. The journal entries regarding him become fewer. Maybe they had a falling out."

"And Lucia?"

"She remains in the household. He mentions their work on several translations, including works in Arabic and Hebrew. He seems fascinated with Kabala, Jewish mysticism, and some Sufi texts from Andalusia."

"So, she's a scholar, not a witch," Giancarlo stated suggestively.

"She's definitely a scholar, but their work in Kabala and Sufism suggests a mystical bend. She might not be your ordinary household herbalist or spell weaver, but she is well versed in mysticism."

"When do you finish your research?"

"I have access to the journal until next week and then it gets returned to the Knights."

"And you'll be returned to us?" Giancarlo said with an imploring look.

"Yes, I promise. You'll have my undivided attention. Maybe we can go to the shore for an early spring getaway."

"What about the mountains? The snow is still good," Giancarlo suggested.

"What would we do with Francesco?"

"We could leave him with Maria for a few days. She would love that, as long as it wasn't too long."

"That's not a bad idea. It would be great to get Luca back on the slopes to reinforce what he learned in January, and I wouldn't mind taking some time in the mountains. I miss winter living in Rome."

"I'll look into some dates and accommodations, and I'll speak with Maria."

"I think you have access to my calendar. Just work around the tours I'm giving."

11

Chapter Eleven – The Grimoire

The next day, after giving a morning tour of the Vatican Museums, Oliver made his way to the library. It was his last day with the journal, and he was ready to wrap up his study.

He took his reserved seat and opened the protective box for the cardinal's journal. He found his bookmark and began to decipher new notations. They were shorter, and the script was not as easy to read, suggesting that the cardinal's hands had become shaky. There were references to his being ill and the household staff taking care of him.

He acknowledged that he was nearing death and made instructions about the liquidation of his estate. There was a notation about sending funds to Florence to support Francesco. And there was a scribbled mention of Lucia. Oliver had trouble making sense of it but eventually concluded that she was to return to the Institute. The cardinal paid Madre a stipend to take care of Lucia, and he gave Lucia several of his prized books, including a grimoire that he noted had been hers originally.

The journal ended abruptly, apparently with Salviati's death.

Oliver did more research on Francesco. Apparently, he died 10 years later. He had returned to Rome. There is little information on where he lived or what he was doing in Rome at the time. He was unable to find more information on Luz or Lucia Ruiz.

Oliver had mixed feelings as he closed the journal. He was glad to finish the project, but he had grown fond of Salviati, Francesco, and Lucia, and wanted to know more about their lives and how things ended. He made his way to the director's desk and let him know he had concluded his work. He thanked him and made his way out to the Borgo area, where he grabbed a quick panino and coffee.

It was a cool, overcast day. Oliver took the long walk home. He crossed the Ponte Sant' Angelo, a beautiful bridge built by Hadrian to connect ancient Rome with his tomb on the other side of the river. He meandered along the quiet medieval streets, all pedestrian areas since Rome rid its center of choking traffic and pollution. He took the path that would lead to the Campo de' Fiori, the large open-air market. Along the narrow road, he passed small workshops where craftsmen repaired furniture, rewired lamps, restored paintings, and sold antiques. He came upon an antique book dealer and walked inside.

The owner looked up over the top of a book he was reading and asked if he could be of assistance. At first, Oliver said he was just browsing. But then he asked, "By any chance do you have, or have you come across any grimoires?"

The man's face lit up. He responded, "Most people don't even know what a grimoire is. Is there a particular one you have in mind?"

"No. Although I am interested in grimoires that might have been in circulation in the 1500s."

"Ah, well, that's going to be quite rare. I've never seen anything like that. Every once-in-a-while, I will get a copy of magic books from England – dating from the 1700s and 1800s – but nothing earlier."

The shopkeeper rubbed his chin and looked off in the distance and then said, "There's a collector here in Rome who might have something like that. An odd sort of man, if you ask me. His name is Etienne Brome. He's from the south of France."

"Do you have any contact information for him, or is there a way for me to get a message to him?"

"Let me have your contact information, and I will see if he might have something to show you."

Oliver wrote his phone number and email address on a small card and handed it to the owner. The owner examined the information carefully, looked up at Oliver, and smiled. "We'll be in touch."

Oliver left the shop and texted Paola, letting her know he could swing by and pick up Francesco and Luca. He buzzed her building, and she invited him to come upstairs.

"How were they today?"

"Luca just arrived a couple of hours ago from school. He had lunch and was taking a nap when you texted. Francesco has been good. He took a nap this morning, and he's ready for a feeding when you get home."

"Thanks for taking such good care of them?"

"It's my pleasure. They are incredibly easy to care for. Whatever you guys are going, it's working."

Oliver smiled. He put Francesco into a sling close to his chest. He took Luca's hand, and they began the short walk home. Once inside, Luca went back to his nap. He fed Francesco and then laid him in his bed. Oliver opened his computer, checked emails, and attend to some correspondence.

Later, Giancarlo arrived. He was in a good mood, having landed another lucrative account for the bank. He had picked up a bottle of Prosecco from a local grocer to celebrate. They opened the bottle and poured it into a couple of glasses and toasted each other.

"Cheers!" they said in unison.

"Congratulations," Oliver added. "Does this mean we can go on the ski trip next week?"

"Yes. We can stay in a nice place, and we can buy some skis and equipment."

Oliver smiled. Luca wandered down from his room, giving Giancarlo a big hug. "How's your brother?" Giancarlo asked.

"He's still asleep. I checked in on him," Luca said in a very adult-like fashion.

"We appreciate that," Oliver said.

"So, how was your day?" Giancarlo asked Oliver.

"Good. I finished the research. I was a bit melancholy giving up the journal, and I don't have any more information on Francesco or Lucia."

Giancarlo sighed, relieved that Oliver's chase for evidence connecting Luca and Francesco with 16th century people was over. He was looking forward to simple pleasures of dinner, walks in the neighborhood, occasional excursions to the family villa, and skiing in the Alps.

"There is one lead I still want to pursue," Oliver interjected. Giancarlo creased his forehead. "There's reference to a grimoire, an esoteric book - perhaps a book of magic - in the cardinal's notes. The book belonged to Lucia. He gave it to her when he sent her back to the Institute."

"And?" Giancarlo inquired.

"Well, I stopped in an antique bookshop on my way back from the Vatican. The owner mentioned a collector in town that might be able to help me find it or something like it."

Giancarlo took a long sip of Prosecco. "If you weren't so cute, I would have lost patience a long time ago with this – what do you say in English – wild goose chase?"

Oliver smiled and gave Giancarlo a kiss. "It's not a wild goose chase. Think about it – we identified one of the former owners of our house who was a prominent 16th century cardinal and part of the Medici clan. We uncovered a romantic attachment between him and a prominent artist – who happens to share the same name with our son. And we learned that the cardinal employed a scholar named Lucia, who happens to have been accused by some of being a sorcerer."

"It is an interesting tale, but the connections between our Francesco and our Luca are coincidental. *Basta*. Story closed."

"We'll see," Oliver stated emphatically. "But, for the time being, I want chocolate, wine, and sex!"

"What about dinner first?"

"It's in the oven. How does a roast chicken sound?"

"Is it Anna's recipe? Whenever I see the chicken with the sprigs of rosemary wedged in its wings, I have heart palpitations," Giancarlo said with alarm.

Oliver creased his forehead and stared at Giancarlo inquisitively.

"It was what your mothers served the night of the inquisition."

"It wasn't an inquisition. They were just anxious about us."

"They were ready to chase me out of Boston. They were not happy that their son had just come out, was only 20, and had decided to move in with a 30-year-old banker in Rome."

"You have to admit, it was a lot for them or anyone to process. But they adore you now!"

"I was on probation for a couple of years, If I recall."

"You're not only out of probation, but you're their favorite."

"No, their favorites are Francesco and Luca. We are just caretakers."

"Speaking of – can you help Luca into his chair and then get Francesco? Let's feed him while we're all eating."

Giancarlo helped Luca into his chair, went upstairs, and returned with Francesco. He grinned when he saw Luca at the table, and he babbled something.

Oliver took the chicken out of the oven, placed it on a platter, and strained the ravioli which he coated in a little butter and parmesan cheese. They sat at the table and enjoyed dinner.

The next morning, Luca was at school and Francesco was taking a nap. Oliver's phone rang, and he answered, "*Pronto.*"

A man with a thick French accent introduced himself. "I'm Etienne, Etienne Brome. I was speaking with Gabi at the bookstore, and he said you were interested in a grimoire from the 16th century. I have several things you might find interesting."

"Really? I was doing research on a 16th century cardinal and his in-house scholar, and I think she inherited a grimoire from her parents who had immigrated from Spain."

"Yes. I have a grimoire from that period. It's written in Arabic, Hebrew, and Castilian. Would you like to take a look?"

"That would be incredible. However, I don't read Arabic or Hebrew."

"Me neither, but I have a contact in town who does. We can talk."

Etienne gave Oliver his address. A couple of days later, Oliver made his way to Etienne's apartment, just around the corner from the Piazza Navona. Oliver rang the bell and Etienne buzzed him in. Oliver climbed a broad marble staircase to a landing where a large antique door was open. As he approached, an older man, perhaps in his 70s, stepped into the light streaming from inside the apartment.

"Welcome. I'm Etienne," the man said, extending his pale hands and long bony fingers in a timid handshake.

"I'm Oliver. Nice to meet you."

"Come in."

Etienne stepped back as Oliver walked into the sunny space. "Can I offer you something to drink – tea, coffee, water, or juice?"

"No, thank you. I'm fine."

"Have a seat," Etienne pointed to an antique sofa in the center of the large room. The ceilings were high and painted in astrological motifs. The room was long and oval, with a large bay window on the far side. On the right side of the room, there were several carved chairs set between tall Chinese armoires. On the left side of the room were floor to ceiling wooden shelves filled with old books. Etienne sat opposite Oliver in a large, cushioned chaise. He wore a long, dark blue silk house coat over dark pants, a white dress shirt, and a long scarf draped around his neck. He had long, gray, wavy hair resting on his shoulders. He had the look of a professor, artist, and an eccentric wealthy man all in one.

He looked intensely at Oliver with his piercing green eyes and said, "So, you are interested in a particular grimoire."

Oliver cleared his throat and said, "Yes. I was doing some research on a cardinal in the 16th century here in Rome. He had engaged a woman to translate works for him, and she apparently had inherited the grimoire from her father."

"And why are you interested in the grimoire?" Etienne asked in a slow, deliberate voice.

Oliver was at a loss for what to reply. "Hmm, well, I was hoping it might fill in some blanks."

Etienne leaned back in his chair, crossed his legs, and nodded. "What blanks?"

Oliver was uneasy with Etienne's intense look and curiosity, and he wondered if he had made a mistake in coming. Etienne noticed his hesitancy and added, "I'm sorry for being intrusive. It's not too often that I meet someone who is interested in grimoires, much less a particular one."

"You collect them?"

"Yes, amongst other things. Come look," he said in a certain ironic tone. He stood and pointed toward the bookcase.

Oliver approached the case and marveled at the variety of manuscripts in different bindings, script, color, and size. He asked, "What inspired your interest in historical books?"

"My mother inherited a collection from her grandmother. She died when I was young, and I maintained my connection to her through these books."

"And your father?"

"Oh, he couldn't have been bothered. He was a businessman. He indulged me. I think he felt guilty when my mother died, and he remarried."

Oliver tilted his head and deciphered some of the titles. "It looks like you have a lot of interest in archaeology from what I see here."

"Yes. I'm surprised you can make sense of the labels."

"I studied archaeology."

Etienne's face lit up.

"And you said you collect grimoires. Where are they?"

"I keep them in a special cabinet." Etienne looked toward the side of the bookcase to a glass enclosed wooden case. Oliver followed his glance.

Etienne walked toward the case and took a key out of his pocket, unlocking the door. A musty odor wafted through the air as he pulled the doors back. He pulled out a book with wooden covers and a latch. Oliver's eyes widened.

"Most people think of something like this when they think of a grimoire – a compendium of spells locked in a wooden binder."

Oliver nodded; his eyes opened wide.

Etienne suspected Oliver had little familiarity with grimoires or magic and continued, "There are all sorts of texts that we might refer to as esoteric works."

Oliver smiled and said, "Like the Gnostics in early Christianity?"

"Precisely!" Etienne said excitedly, now realizing Oliver might be better versed than he thought. "Most of those were lost, but we have references to them and, now with the Nag Hamadi scrolls, we have some of the originals."

"You don't have any of them, do you?" Oliver asked, wondering how important Etienne's collection might be.

Etienne nodded no. "This is the book I treasure the most," he said as he held out an old manuscript. "It's an original copy of the *Hermeticum*, translated into Latin by Marsilio Ficino." Etienne waited for Oliver's response.

"Wow! How incredible to see an original," Oliver said excitedly. The *Hermeticum* was a collection of ancient texts that was translated by Ficino in the 15th century into Latin. It sparked great interest in alchemy and magic and was part of a broader interest in resurrecting ancient Greek philosophy.

Oliver continued, "I've always been fascinated with that period – when artists, philosophers, and politicians all seemed to have appeared at the same time to recreate an ancient age. Think of Michelangelo, Ficino, and the Medicis! How did all of that talent and thought come together?"

"And then what happened?" Etienne asked.

"What do you mean?"

"Well, you have this golden age of the Platonic Academy and great art and architecture – then poof – it all gets shut down."

Oliver looked perplexed. Etienne continued, "By the middle of the 1500s, you have these narrow-minded autocrats – like Pope Paul IV – who persecuted heretics, witches, and people of other religious persuasion. Books like the *Hermeticum* were forbidden because they were associated with magic," Etienne said with an odd gleam in his eye.

"Wasn't Paul IV originally Gian Pietro Carafa?"

Etienne nodded nervously. "How do you know that?"

"Well, I'm a guide. I have to know that history."

"I know, but I detect a bit more familiarity than usual."

"Well, he's part of the blanks I'm hoping to fill."

"Ah ha," Etienne said, replacing the books in the case. He reached for another and pulled it out. "I believe this is the one you're looking for."

Oliver took hold of a well-preserved book bound in burgundy leather. He felt a flow of heat race up his arms as he opened the cover. He noticed the Arabic lettering and looked up at Etienne with disappointment.

"I know. I wish I could read Arabic as well." He took the book back and flipped through the pages. "Look at these symbols with Arabic and Hebrew text underneath. I'm curious what it says."

"This is amazing. How long have you had this?"

"It was part of my mother's collection. I assume she inherited it from her mother. It's a family heirloom."

Oliver wondered why Etienne had never had someone translate it for him. He asked, "You've never explored it with a translator?"

"No. I had other grimoires that piqued my curiosity earlier. I kept thinking I would get to it. Over the years, books have made their way to me mysteriously. I believe there's some kind of fate or providence that leads us to the books we need. Perhaps the book was waiting for you," he said with a wink.

What Etienne didn't disclose to Oliver was that he had tried to decipher the text, but only certain parts were intelligible. There were large sections of text that appeared to be Hebrew or Arabic, but even with translators, they were indecipherable. He suspected the book only disclosed itself fully to those who were part of a particular lineage, and he sensed Oliver might be part of it.

Oliver felt unnerved. He then asked, "What do you know about it in general?"

"Only that it was first produced in Andalusia in the late 1300s, perhaps by Jewish mystics. It is unique in that I arranged it much like the Talmud."

"Wow," Oliver remarked as he turned the pages and noticed the format. "There must be incredible accumulated wisdom here."

Etienne nodded. "And look here," he added. "There are a series of reflections or notes by owners of the book. Most include a date. They are in a variety of languages."

Oliver scrutinized the pages as Etienne flipped them, presuming they were Hebrew, Arabic, Castilian, and Latin entries, names, and dates. "Is there a Lucia?"

Etienne flipped to the last entries. They were in Italian. "It looks like the last notes were made by a Loretta in 1890."

"What about earlier?"

Etienne worked backward. "Before Loretta there was another set of Italian notes by Luna and, before her, a Luca."

Oliver's heart pounded as he heard the name Luca. "What year were the Luca notes?"

"Looks like they were in the first part of the 1800s. Why?"

"Just curious," Oliver replied, concealing his fascination.

"The earlier notes then shift to Hebrew and then to Arabic."

"Can you determine names?"

Etienne nodded no.

"Dates?"

"A few. Here's one from 1490 in Castilian. There's a long break until 1555. It's interesting. With that notation, in Arabic, there are three dates: 962- 5315-1555. If it were my guess, this would be the year 1555 and the same year in Islamic and Jewish calendars."

Oliver thought to himself, Cardinal Salviati died in 1553, and the Jewish ghetto was created by Pope Paul IV in 1555. If this was Lucia's grimoire, maybe these were the last entries she made.

"Do you know anyone who reads Arabic?"

"In fact, I do. She's a bit eccentric."

Oliver thought the statement was ironic and asked, "In what sense?"

"Well, Rahel dabbles in the arts."

"What arts?"

"Well, she does readings and such."

"Hmm. That's probably not a problem if she's going to translate a grimoire."

Etienne raised his brows.

"Can we engage her? I would be happy to take care of the cost."

Etienne nodded. He had already written her information on a small card and handed it to Oliver. "I expected you would want someone to decipher the text for you. Here's Rahel's address and phone number. And here's the grimoire. Please guard it with your life."

Etienne extended his hand with the grimoire to Oliver. As Oliver took hold of the book, he felt Etienne tug slightly, as if he were reluctant to release it. Etienne looked intensely at Oliver and said, "You are quite exotic, you know. Dark complexion, blonde hair, and blue eyes."

Oliver wasn't sure if Etienne was making a pass or just making an observation. Self-consciously he replied, "Yes, my biological parents were French and Scandinavian."

"Your biological parents?"

"Yes. I was adopted."

"Do your parents live in Rome?"

"No. They are in Boston."

"And how did you end up in Rome?" Etienne pressed.

Oliver looked hesitant to respond. Etienne seemed eager to engage Oliver further. He said, "Why don't you have a seat? I can make some tea."

Oliver nodded timidly. Etienne went around the corner into a kitchen and boiled some water. He returned with a set of porcelain cups and tea bags and, when the kettle whistled, retrieved it, and brought it into the parlor.

"So, I'm curious. How did you end up in Rome?"

Oliver hesitated, not sure what Etienne's cultural and political views might be. He didn't want to lose the opportunity to explore the grimoire. He said matter-of-factly, "I came to study archaeology."

"Ah," Etienne murmured as he looked at Oliver's hand and noticed the ring. "And you married here?"

"Yes," Oliver said without elaboration.

"I'm still fascinated by your interest in a grimoire," Etienne said without further specification, leaving an opening for Oliver to continue.

"Well, I found some notes while renovating my home. They belonged to a cardinal who, as I mentioned, had engaged a woman to translate manuscripts for him. She inherited a grimoire from her father. I was curious to see if I could find it."

"That doesn't explain your personal interest," Etienne noted with a grin and intense look.

Oliver cleared his throat. "I have a son who has a vivid imagination."

"Is that what you call it?" Etienne said thoughtfully, crossing his legs as if to settle into an even longer exchange with Oliver.

Oliver nodded.

"And your son, in what sense does he have a vivid imagination?" Etienne continued.

"The usual. Imaginary friends and unrecognizable languages."

"Go on."

"Well," Oliver began, leaning on the edge of his seat, "he seems to be able to influence weather, and he is oddly prescient – like he knows when something is about to happen."

Etienne nodded and smiled contently. He was now optimistic that Oliver or Oliver's son might be part of the lineage of the book and capable of deciphering it with Rahel's help.

Etienne nodded again and then said, "How old is your son?"

"Nearly five. He's grown so quickly."

"I'm sure he has," Etienne said. "And your wife? Is she curious?"

Oliver shifted in place. This was the information he didn't want to share. Etienne noticed his reticence and said, "Oh, I'm sorry for making you uncomfortable. I shouldn't be coy. I know you are married to a man."

Oliver looked askance at him. "How?"

"I looked you up before you came. I wouldn't have invited you without some sense of who you were. I have to say, this makes me more comfortable."

"In what sense?"

"You know what it's like to be marginalized, to feel the shame projected onto you by various institutions. If you are going to study a grimoire, you must be willing to put up with the scorn people will have for you studying magic. As a gay man, you've learned how to deal with that."

Oliver scrutinized Etienne more carefully. Within the folds of his silk robe and dress shirt, he noticed a pendent hanging from his neck – a quartz crystal nestled in a silver holder. Over Etienne's shoulder, he noticed, for the first time, a bowl of rough amethyst stones. He followed his eyes up the wall and to the elaborate astrological motifs on the ceiling. Initially he thought they were older paintings but now wondered if Etienne had them painted, perhaps in some kind of constellation favorable to him. He now began to wonder if Etienne was a sorcerer and, perhaps, even a gay one.

"Yes. I recognize how judgmental people can be, and how ignorant they are," Oliver said.

Etienne sighed contently. "I look forward to what you learn from Rahel."

"Me, too," Oliver said excitedly. He looked at his watch and said, "I think I have taken enough of your time. I appreciate your generosity in letting me study the grimoire. I will take good care of it."

"I know you will. Besides, it has a protective spell on it."

Oliver stared at Etienne as if he had seen a ghost. He wasn't sure he wanted to bring something that had a spell on it into his home.

Etienne noticed Oliver's anxiousness and said, "I'm just kidding. But please be careful with it."

"I will. And I will call after Rahel and I visit."

Etienne showed Oliver to the door, and Oliver walked back out into the mid-day Roman light.

12

Chapter Twelve – Rahel

A few days later, Oliver knocked on the door of a first-floor apartment in a dense neighborhood not far from the Trevi fountain. A woman unlatched the door and opened it, standing in the dim light of the foyer.

"*Benvenuto*," she said, welcoming Oliver inside.

The woman was about 50. She had black hair, dark caramel complexion, brown eyes, and dark red lips. She smiled. Her teeth were bright white and in perfect condition. She had a radiance to her, and Oliver felt instantly enchanted.

She introduced herself, "I'm Rahel, and you must be Oliver."

Oliver reached out to shake her hand. She seemed hesitant to touch Oliver's hand, but eventually did so. She looked at Oliver up and down as he walked through the doorway. She seemed intrigued by the book Oliver held in his hand.

She led him into her apartment and invited him to take a seat in a large chair. She sat opposite him. The chairs circled a low, round coffee table and were set on top of a deep red and blue Persian carpet. A few table lamps lit the room dimly.

Oliver began, "Thank you for agreeing to consider translating this grimoire."

"Yes, Mr. Brome contacted me."

"I have been doing research on Rome in the 16th century," Oliver began.

"Yes, I know. You are curious about your children," she began.

Oliver creased his forehead and said, "How do you know that?"

"I just do."

"Etienne says you are a reader," Oliver continued.

She nodded.

"And you know Arabic and Hebrew?" Oliver inquired.

"I'm from Morocco. Since I was raised a Jew, I learned Hebrew. We spoke Arabic at home, and my family worked in tourism, so I learned Spanish as well."

"When did you come to Italy?"

"About ten years ago, when my father immigrated. Can I see the book?" she asked, wanting to move beyond pleasantries.

Oliver handed her the book. She trembled as she took hold of it. She murmured, "It's very powerful."

Oliver leaned forward, eager to observe her interaction with it.

She flipped through the pages, sighing from time to time and nodding her head. She ran her fingers over several of the symbols and mouthed some of the words as she read the text.

"So, can you help me with it?"

She nodded. She continued to flip through the pages. "This is an interesting book. I've never seen anything like it. It looks like the Talmud and includes commentary from people over many generations."

Oliver looked lost. Rahel explained, "On each page of the Talmud, there is a passage from the Torah around which are printed the interpretations of rabbinical scholars over the ages. There's always a blank section of the page showing that there is still more to uncover or understand of the passage. This has the same format – a passage or symbol or spell and then surrounding commentary."

"So, is this a magical Torah?"

"Not exactly." She turned some pages and scanned the text. "There are some passages from the Torah and from the Qur'an – a blend of Kabala and Sufism. But here," she continued, "is a spell. And this page includes a more theoretical reflection. There are also interesting symbols, perhaps formulas for creating sacred space or for setting particular intentions."

"Are any commentaries recent?"

Rahel turned to a page and tilted her head to read the smaller notes around a passage. "Strange," she murmured. She squinted her eyes, ran her fingers over the text, tilted her head again and repeated, "Very strange."

"What?"

"Some of the text makes sense, but other parts don't. There are sections where the script is clearly Hebrew or Arabic. But when I try to read it, the section looks like a jumble of characters. I can't detect actual words or phrases."

"Is it a dialect of Hebrew or Arabic?"

"I don't think so. I'm versed in most of the major dialects, and from a distance, the script looks normal. But when one gets closer, it changes."

"What do you think that means?"

"If I were to guess, I would say that the book only discloses itself to particular individuals or perhaps to individuals who know how to open it with a spell."

Oliver looked dejected.

"Don't worry," she added. "If the book has landed in your lap, I have a feeling it was meant to, and we will find a way to decipher it. Look at this list of previous owners who have written personal messages in the back. The book is waiting for a new owner."

Oliver now looked alarmed.

"Don't be frightened. It is a good book. But it has an energy to it. It's as if it is alive and active in selecting and preserving a lineage."

"A lineage of what?"

"Sorcerers, wizards, witches – the wise ones."

Again, Oliver's eyes widened, and he remained silent.

"I'm curious about someone named Lucia. Someone from the 1500s."

Rahel turned several pages, exploring the noted commentaries. She nodded no. She turned to the back of the book and read the reflections of various owners. "There's an LR who writes something in 1555. Is that who you are looking for?"

"Probably. Lucia had been named Luz Ruiz. It might be helpful to know what she wrote and if there are other notations in the book from her."

"It will take me some time to explore the book and jot down some notes, at least from the parts I can read. Should we set a date for you to return?"

"How much time do you need?"

"Why don't we meet in a week? Next Thursday?"

"Perfect," Oliver said, looking nervously at the book.

"Oh, I'll take good care of it. Not to worry."

"You noticed my hesitancy, huh?"

Rahel nodded.

They bowed to each other. Rahel showed Oliver to the door, and he stepped out into the cool air and made his way home.

A week later, Oliver and Rahel sat opposite each other in the center of her parlor. She handed him several pages of notes corresponding to various pages of the grimoire.

"First, I looked for commentaries reflecting dates in the 1500s and LR. There are several which I have noted. I also translated LR's remarks at the end of the book. In addition, I selected some passages that I found interesting, particularly considering LR's reflections."

Oliver glanced over the pages, eager to glean as much as he could about Lucia and, perhaps, his son. "Any highlights?"

"Well, LR is a woman, and she had been under the protection of Cardinal Salviati."

"Wow! The book actually includes that information? That's amazing confirmation! She must be Lucia."

Rahel nodded and smiled broadly. "Yes. Apparently, she did translations for him, and they had philosophical discussions."

"And?"

"From what I can piece together, LR or Lucia inherited the book from her father, who had received it from his mother. She was arrested, and the book was confiscated, but Salviati retrieve it and return it to her."

"Fascinating!"

"Yes, I imagine this is helping you put a lot of pieces together."

Oliver nodded.

"At the end of the book, Lucia is frustrated and fearful. She believes she will be arrested again, and that the Pope will confiscate the book – perhaps even burn it."

"If the last notations from Lucia are in 1555, the Cardinal has already died. Lucia is probably back in the Institute with the grimoire and perhaps fearful that Pope Paul IV will take revenge on the freedom she enjoyed under Salviati's protection," Oliver suggested.

"Yes. She mentions that. She is also angry and frustrated."

"About?"

"About the failure of magic."

Oliver looked curiously at Rahel, who continued. "She was frustrated that the spells didn't work earlier."

"Which ones?"

"A love spell and a protection spell."

"Who did she put a love spell on?"

"Isn't it obvious? Cardinal Salviati."

"And it didn't work?"

"She laments that he was in love with the artist."

Oliver's eyes widened. "That must be Francesco."

"She puts a protective spell on herself and the book after Salviati's death, but she fears the Pope is closing in on her and will take the book."

"So, after 1555, we don't have anything else from Lucia or anyone else until when?"

"1705, in the Kingdom of Naples. And it is quite fascinating what I found. The owner after LR writes, 'I acquired *Kashf* from a local bookdealer who had been trying to sell it. When I walked into the shop, the book fell off the shelf. He picked it up and set it on the counter. I was looking for a copy of the *Hermeticum*, which he didn't have. He asked me if I might be interested in something similar, and he showed me the book. When I took hold of it, I could feel heat in my hands. I knew Arabic and, at once, recognized the value of the book and bought it. When I took it home, I read the reflections of the previous owners and detected the disappointment of LR. *Kashf* ended up being protected, after all. It is in perfect shape. I get a feeling from the book that LR was saved by someone. Our intentions or imagination work, but they don't always work as we expect.'"

"Who wrote that?"

"Bartolomeo Vescovo."

"Doesn't that mean bishop?"

"Yes. *Vescovo* could be a surname, but it could be a way for this Bartolomeo to leave his clerical status ambiguous."

"I can't imagine a Catholic cleric being a sorcerer."

"Well, in fact, many were. There are many grimoires that have been found in monastic collections, showing a keen interest in magic amongst the more educated clergy."

"Who owned the book after Bartolomeo?"

"A certain Carmela. She was one of Bartolomeo's students.

"He had students? As in a school for witches?"

"Yes. And he notes how he was guided to bequeath the grimoire to her. The book seems to be protected and always falls into the right hands."

Oliver raised his brows and Rahel added, "Yes, that means you."

"I'm not a sorcerer."

"Maybe you are, and you don't realize it yet. Or maybe this is for your son."

Over felt a current of warm air rush over his collar as she said that. Rahel looked straight into his eyes and said, "There's a lot of karma between your two sons."

"What do you mean?"

"I'm not sure, but I sense there's a connection with this grimoire and there's something they have to work out."

Oliver nodded, recalling what Luca had told his mom.

"You mentioned Lucia was frustrated. Do you think she didn't know what she was doing?"

"Since there's a gap between an entry in 1490 and hers in the mid-1500s, I suspect Lucia didn't have any coaches or mentors and probably learned of her lineage late in life."

Oliver looked curious, so Rahel continued, "But even so, magic is not a matter of simply following spells correctly, and Lucia doesn't seem to understand that."

"Tell me more," Oliver said.

"Magic is about setting intentions, using one's imagination to envision something."

Oliver nodded as if he understood, but it was all new to him.

"We cast our imagination in a matrix full of other people's intentions. Think of it as a surface full of waves that intersect. Some waves cancel other waves out. Some waves get amplified by other waves. When waves intersect, new patterns emerge. Many people today use the language of energy to describe this. Our consciousness is essentially a vehicle for radiating and receiving energy."

"I've heard people talk about empaths, people who are more in tune with emotions and thoughts around them," Oliver suggested.

"Hmm, hum," Rahel said. "That's what a reader is. A reader or a psychic is someone who has learned to trust his or her intuition and listen to the messages he or she receives. We all have it, but we are often taught as children to distrust our vibes."

Oliver thought of Luca and wondered what messages he was already picking up that led him to mistrust his intuition.

"Sorcery or magic is learning how to be clear about one's intentions and create the conditions where those intentions will be amplified and supported. Spells are ways of setting intention and surrounding them with the emotions that support them. Symbols and actions such as lighting candles, combining herbs, using gestures, and things like that are interchangeable. There's nothing inherently potent about one symbol or gesture or another. What is potent is the intention and the belief in its power."

"Fascinating," Oliver remarked. "So, magic isn't about conjuring demons or spirits to do our work?"

"That was a big debate in Medieval and Renaissance times. Islam, Judaism, and Christianity all condemned demonic magic. But there were many philosophers and religious leaders who believed there was natural magic or magic that simply worked with energy. They often spoke of it in terms of astrological magic, the influence of the planets which, if you think about it, is nothing more than energy."

"Weren't there witches or wizards who invoked demons?"

"Yes, and perhaps there are malevolent spirits – or even good ones - that can amplify intentions. But my belief is that demons or spirits are ways for sorcerers to trust their intentions or desires. It is a way of believing they are powerful – which is essentially how it all works."

"My son?" Oliver began tentatively.

"Yes, I was waiting for you to bring him up," Rahel interjected.

"He seems to have a very vivid imagination, as my husband suggests."

Rahel nodded. "Continue."

"Well, is he a sorcerer or just someone with a vivid imagination?"

"What's the difference?" Rahel asked. "Isn't sorcery a matter of casting imagination out into the world and clothing it with positive emotions?"

"I never thought of it that way. For example, my son seems to be able to change weather."

"All the time?" she inquired.

"Most of the time, but not always."

"He undoubtedly imagines a certain outcome and clothes it with positive feelings – perhaps feelings about what he wants to do or, in other cases, out of concern for the delight of others."

Oliver thought of Luca's interest in creating conditions for his cousins to go to the beach or for the two of them to take a walk.

"But sometimes forces are already set in motion, and no amount of good intention or imagination can change them. That doesn't mean magic doesn't work, it just reinforces the idea that magic works within a matrix of other forces, intentions, and other people's imagination."

Oliver nodded. He rubbed his chin and then leaned toward Rahel and asked, "Rahel. I have a question to ask."

She nodded for him to continue.

"What about past lives?"

"What about them?" she inquired.

"Well, in your opinion, do they exist?"

"Most certainly."

"My son seems to be aware of things from a previous existence."

"At early ages, a child's ego formation is still in flux, and it is possible for some to be more aware of previous lives, particularly if they are bringing into this life significant issues to resolve or face."

"What should I do?"

"What do you mean?" Rahel asked.

Oliver was stumped. "I don't know – I feel as though things are happening that I should pay attention to."

"That's always a good strategy," she said with a smile.

"No, I mean strange things."

She nodded for him to continue.

"Why did we end up in the house we did? Why does my son seem familiar with the house? Why does he seem already to know his brother who, he claims, was an artist? Why did we find the cardinal's journals and information about a grimoire – which, against all odds, we found as well? Where is all of this leading?"

"The title of this book might be a first clue – *Kashf*."

Oliver looked lost.

"The unveiling. Most of us live in the dark, out of touch with deeper things that are happening."

Oliver nodded for her to continue.

"Whoever Lucia was, she and the cardinal seemed to have been on a quest for knowledge, for wisdom. Perhaps if there is a connection between Lucia and your son and you, the journey is continuing."

"That makes sense to me. But how?"

"For some reason, this book has landed in your lap. I think you're already sensitive to the notion of synchronicity – the idea that certain events or coincidences are more meaningful than they might be otherwise. There are a lot of things falling into place in your life. Pay attention to them. Pursue them. They will lead you to new understanding."

"But practically speaking, what does that mean?"

"Since part of the book seems to be concealed – and I confirmed that this week - it would be interesting to find out if your son can read it."

"But he doesn't read Arabic or Hebrew or anything much, for that matter. He's only 5."

"Are you sure he won't be able to read it?"

Oliver looked off into the distance and nodded no.

"I'd like to try an experiment. Can you bring Luca here? I'd like to hold him on my lap and try to read the concealed parts of the book with him."

"I think we can do that. Why not?"

"Are you free tomorrow?"

Oliver nodded cautiously, still anxious about involving his son in magic.

13

Chapter Thirteen – Lineage

Oliver held Luca's hand as they walked down several narrow streets towards Rahel's apartment. Luca was carefree, glancing at merchants putting things out on the streets and petting dogs as their owners took morning strolls.

Oliver was anxious, having fought with Giancarlo the night before about exposing Luca to a psychic. Both dug in their heels, and Giancarlo left for work with a punishing silence. They rarely fought. There were little idiosyncrasies that grated on each other's nerves, but generally they had similar tastes and preferences. With Luca, they had always been on the same page, although Oliver was stricter, and Giancarlo could be a pushover when Luca pleaded for something. This was the first time they had each walked away from a fight without agreement or resolution. Oliver felt terrible but was resolved to honor his son's gifts and identity. He hoped Giancarlo would come around.

As they approached Rahel's door, Oliver could feel his heart pound. He looked down at his son, who looked up at him with calm and an endearing smile.

Rahel opened the door just as Oliver was about to knock. "Come in," she said warmly, reaching down to shake Luca's hand. "You must be Luca. I've heard so many good things about you."

"*Piacere*," he said gleefully.

"Would you like some milk and cookies?" she asked Luca.

He nodded.

She showed him a seat in the parlor and brought out a tray with cookies, croissants, and milk. "Let me get some water," she said to Oliver. "I'm going to have tea. Would you like some?"

Oliver nodded yes.

The grimoire was set on the coffee table. Rahel was curious if Luca might recognize it. He took a big gulp of milk and chased it with a cookie, all-the-while glancing at the book. His legs were rocking contently.

"Luca, your dad says you like to read books. I have a book I wanted to read, and I was wondering if you could help me."

Luca smiled.

"Can you sit here on my lap while we read it?" Luca looked at his dad, who nodded. He climbed up on Rahel's lap, and she reached for the grimoire. She put it in front of Luca and said, "Why don't you open it up?"

Luca rubbed his right hand over the front of the book. He thumbed through the book as if looking for a particular section. He landed on a pair of pages and said, "*Ecco. Leggiamo questo.*"

The passage Luca suggested they read was in Hebrew with Arabic, Hebrew, and Castilian commentary surrounding it. There was a notation with LR beside it, one Oliver thought might be Lucia (Luz Ruiz) from Cardinal Salviati's household. It was in Arabic. Rahel could read the commentaries, but the original passage didn't reveal itself to her.

She asked, "Can you read it for me?"

Luca nodded no. Then he said, "You can read it to me."

As soon as he invited her to read, the letters seemed to shift, and the text became legible and coherent. Rahel wondered if her eyes had just not focused before, but she suspected that something mysterious had just occurred.

She recited the text out loud in Hebrew, and Luca smiled. He seemed to comprehend what she was saying, nodding as she continued. She asked, "What does it mean?"

"*Si può fare con l'immaginazione*," he said tentatively (that one can do it with imagination).

"*Bravo*," Rahel said.

She read LR's notation in Arabic. It said, "When God imagines, God's imagination is not forceful. It is cast within a vibrational mode of love, inviting the world that is imagined to resonate with God. In the same way, when we imagine something, we can't force the outcome. We cast our desire or imagination into the world and hope that our positive thoughts will invite other realities to resonate with it. A powerful sorcerer is not someone who compels but one that casts a wide net and invites others to share in a good outcome."

She said to Oliver, "There's a commentary by LR dated 1555. It is very conciliatory, recognizing that imagination can only ideally invite resonance. Didn't the Cardinal die in 1553? If so, perhaps Lucia had made peace with how magic works and wasn't able to constrain him to love her."

Oliver nodded and looked at Luca. Luca continued to rock his feet, sitting on Rahel's lap. He reached over to the book and turned pages as if looking for a particular spot. He settled on a particular page with an image, one much like the magician in a deck of Tarot cards. Under the image was a passage in Arabic. Rahel could make out the letters, but they were, again, incoherent in terms of words or phrases. She tried to read the passage, relying on Luca's previous permission to read. She couldn't decipher the text.

She then asked, "Can you read this?"

Luca nodded no and said, "But you can." He looked up at her with a smile.

She looked back down at the page and the words leaped out at her. She read them aloud to Luca. "The magician reaches out in the universe but stands firmly on the ground. The magician links heaven and earth and the four elements – earth, wind, fire, and water. The magician is a weaver, one who brings elements together with creativity and imagination."

Luca nodded and said, "A magician is like an artist."

She smiled and nodded for him to continue.

Luca looked stumped. She looked down at the text and noticed a commentary with LR initials by it. She read it, "A magician is like an artist. An artist has an impression and recreates the impression, weaving together pigment and canvas. A good painting includes darker areas and hues, like the earth. It includes fluidity or transition between different segments of the scene, like water. It includes light, like fire. And it includes movement, like wind. The four elements come together to create the image of a moment in time, and the observer is drawn in and takes part in the artist's imagination. The artist needs to trust his or her instinct, the movement that inspired the image. It is both inspiration and recognition – something that not only sparks the work but something that is already rooted in the ultimate outcome. It is as if the artist or magician already sees the outcome and follows the elements as they come together to manifest it."

Luca said, "Francesco."

Rahel asked, "Did Francesco say this?"

Luca nodded no.

She asked again, "Did you learn this from Francesco?"

Luca nodded yes.

"Your brother Francesco?"

Luca nodded yes.

Oliver leaned forward from the sofa, mouth agape, not sure what to make of his son. It was clear he was Lucia in the 1500s and lived in the same household as the artist Francesco. They seemed to have been at odds over the affections of the Cardinal, but reconciled later, perhaps after he died. Oliver wondered what that meant for them in this life. How much was Luca aware of his past life and of Francesco? Was it good for him to be aware of his past life, or did he need to embrace fully the current incarnation and hold insights and lessons from the past in his unconscious?

Rahel noticed Oliver's consternation and said, "Do you want to take a break? Or do you have questions?"

"Can you and I meet later in the week, alone? I have a lot of questions."

"I'm sure you do," she said with a warm smile. She looked over at Luca, who seemed engrossed in the grimoire, turning pages, and running his fingers over the text. "Why don't we meet on Thursday? Doesn't Luca go to school in the morning? We could meet then."

"Perfect. *Ci vediamo dopo.*"

"Luca, thanks for reading with me. I look forward to seeing you again soon."

Luca slid off Rahel's lap, grazed his hand over the grimoire, as if saying goodbye, and grabbed his father's hand.

"*Andiamo?*" Oliver asked him.

Luca nodded.

14

Chapter Fourteen - Curriculum

Later in the week, Oliver and Rahel met in her apartment.

"I supposed you are overwhelmed by what we discovered earlier when Luca could open the book."

"Yes. I was not inclined to believe in magic or past lives, but I have to say that between what I have observed of Luca over the years and what happened here with the grimoire, I am a believer."

"I have to admit that even I was surprised by what we witnessed."

"What do we do?"

"I think you and your husband have been entrusted with a momentous task. How does one nurture the talents and gifts of one's child?"

"Isn't that what every parent does?"

"Yes, but few face a set of gifts that are so uncommon. There's no guidebook or parenting book you can rely on for this. You're going to have to be enterprising."

"Can you help us?"

Rahel looked off in the distance as if pondering the question. She turned back to Oliver and said, "I don't have any experience. There are all sorts of curricula for languages, science, mathematics, and the arts, but there isn't a curriculum for this."

"But how did you develop your talents?"

"Like most psychics, I spent much of my childhood and adolescence trying to deny or conceal my so-called gifts. At some point, one just gives in and then follows the gifts where they lead."

"Can't we do that with Luca?"

"You could, but that would be a shame. Luca has a unique opportunity to develop his talents before his ego and our culture encourage him to overlook them or suppress them. He could be quite talented if he could learn to use them now. It's like an athlete or musician or artist. If one learns and practices earlier, there's more opportunity to excel than if one begins later in life."

"But I don't want Luca's identity to be restricted to his magical abilities."

"It shouldn't. Whether one is a painter, a musician, a writer, a teacher, a physician or whatever, excellence includes integrating that identity with other information and abilities. One would hope that a surgeon is good at her art but also appreciates history, literature, art, and other things. A well-rounded wizard is one who is also well-educated and has mastered various subjects and arts so that his imagination is rich and multilayered. Otherwise, he risks becoming narrow minded and controlling."

Oliver smiled, confident that Rahel was not only talented but also a wonderful human being.

"So, what do we do?"

"I propose we put our heads together and come up with a curriculum for Luca. Maybe the grimoire will help us, but I think if we focus on helping Luca become more confident of his intuition and imagination, that will be the key."

"I'll need to discuss this with Giancarlo."

Rahel looked concerned.

"I know. He's not likely to be so enthusiastic."

"Let's trust the process," she said. "Maybe he will surprise us."

Later that evening, after they put the kids to bed, Giancarlo and Oliver discussed the idea of Luca learning more about his abilities. The room was filled with tension and Oliver cautiously and diplomatically shared ideas about mentoring or coaching Luca.

"I will not have my son be taught by a fraudulent psychic," Giancarlo said emphatically, his face turning red.

"She's not fraudulent. She's very intuitive and talented," Oliver interjected.

"I don't care. It will not happen."

"But you've seen Luca. He seems to be gifted. I don't want him to lose that," Oliver pleaded.

"All kids are imaginative and, as they grow up, they become more practical. Life requires it."

"But what about creativity and things like that? Doesn't that draw on intuition and imagination? What if he wants to be an artist, a musician, a writer, or an architect?"

"If he has one of those gifts, we can get him lessons or put him in a special school."

"But what if those gifts could be more developed if he didn't lose his initial ease with intuition?"

"I just don't like the idea of a witch coaching my kid. There's something wrong with that."

"Rahel isn't a witch. She's a psychic."

"Psychic or witch, it's the same thing. You're dabbling in the demonic."

"Not necessarily. Rahel never speaks about demons. She speaks as if her gifts are natural and her own."

"She's a gypsy. That's even worse," he added, trying to build a case against her.

"She's not a gypsy. She's a woman from Morocco."

"Same difference," Giancarlo said, taking a long sip of wine from the glass at the counter.

"Now you're scaring me. Gypsies – or Roma as they are called - are not from north Africa. Most are from the Balkans and originally from northern India," Oliver noted.

"Well, a lot of the palm readers are gypsies."

"I don't know where you get that."

"Look at them," Giancarlo said with disgust.

"I have, and most are native Italians, not gypsies."

"This Rahel you keep talking about – that sounds like a gypsy name to me."

"It's Arabic, from Morocco. She was raised Jewish. She's very educated."

"Then why is she reading palms and cards outside in the squares?"

"She happens to be very talented and makes a lot of money doing it. Besides, she finds it difficult to get employment when store owners find out she's from north Africa. They're racists. Why don't we meet with her so you can ask her questions?"

"No. I've made up my mind. I don't want my son to be coached by a witch, palm reader, or anything of the sort. If he's artistic, his talents will prevail."

"What about spirituality?" Oliver pressed.

"What do you mean?"

"Shouldn't Luca learn about spirituality?"

"He's Catholic," Giancarlo asserted.

"He goes to Mass twice a year. He's been to some weddings, baptisms, and funerals. That's not very spiritual."

"He knows the Biblical stories and the commandments."

Oliver stared at Giancarlo. He sighed, not sure what to say next. He waited a few seconds and then formulated a thought. "How does he connect with the larger universe? How does he develop a sense of his own goodness and turn that into love and compassion for others? How does he develop a relationship with God and with other spiritual beings?"

"Maybe we need to go to church more often. Maybe it's time to explore Sunday school for him."

"I'm not opposed to that," Oliver began. "But are you sure you want to expose him to that paradigm?"

"You and your paradigms. What do you mean?" Giancarlo said with consternation.

"The old paradigm that God is in heaven and that we need intermediaries to access him," Oliver said, emphasizing 'him' when he referred to God. "Or the church's views on women and gay people?"

"That's why we don't go anymore."

"So, what do we replace it with?" Oliver asked thoughtfully.

"I don't know. But it's not witchcraft."

"I don't think I have that in mind, either. But the understanding of the world that psychics and mediums and sorcerers have is more in line with my understanding of God and of science. You've even talked about quantum physics and ideas about how consciousness shapes reality."

"I said that?"

"Hmm, hum," Oliver murmured, then he continued, "Rahel is essentially someone who has learned to trust her instincts and intuition. She is good at picking up on people's thoughts and emotions. She helps people become clear about their intentions and use their imagination to help realize their goals. She senses that all of us are connected at some level and that, through our thoughts and intentions, we can help others."

"That doesn't sound so strange," Giancarlo said, rubbing his chin.

"No. It isn't. But someone who is intuitive scares people. Remember the time Luca knew the delivery people were coming early to our house? That freaked me out. I thought, 'this kid is odd, peculiar, possessed.' In fact, he just has a powerful gift of picking up on things. He's intuitive. And it will be easy for him to feel shame about it. We need to help him trust it, be proud of it, and develop it."

"I don't want him waving wands around or casting spells."

"You mean like chasing clouds away with his hands?"

"Yes. I don't mind if he has a powerful imagination, but I'm not comfortable with him thinking he can control weather or move objects or things like that."

"What are you most concerned with – his imagination or your embarrassment at him waving his hands at the clouds in public?"

Giancarlo blushed. He realized he was embarrassed by his son's overt efforts to influence things, but he wasn't sure how to answer Oliver.

"Maybe he could conceal it a bit," he said, looking away to avoid Oliver's glance.

"So, you're okay with him using his imagination?"

"I don't know what harm there is in it, as long as he doesn't set his expectations too high. I still think most of it is a coincidence."

"I find it hard to believe, too. But over the past year, it has become increasingly difficult to deny that something is going on. There are too many times when his premonitions are right, his intuition is on target, and what he imagines happens. He has an extra sense or something that is worth supporting."

"I just don't want him to be teased or the subject of scorn. He's already had to face this with gay fathers. I don't want it to be worse for him," Giancarlo expressed passionately.

"As gay men, we are both all too aware of that. That's even more reason to help him develop confidence in himself and pride about his identity."

"But it's one thing to develop pride about being gay. That's something real, something biological, something that is incontrovertible. Being a wizard is pure fantasy. It's the product of a wild imagination, fairy tales, fiction. It's okay for kids to pretend, but it's not real. Luca needs to grow out of it."

Oliver's heart sunk. He realized he and Giancarlo faced an immense chasm between them, a line in the sand that was being drawn. He was increasingly convinced there was something real and substantial to Luca's abilities and his connection to Lucia in Salviati's household. Given the progress of the last decades, Oliver couldn't imagine parents rejecting the sexual identity of their children. He now realized he and Giancarlo were on the cutting edge of a whole new cultural phenomenon, accepting psychic abilities in their children.

Desperate to help Luca accept his abilities, Oliver asked, "What if we compromised?"

"In what sense?"

"What if Rahel taught me, and I taught Luca? Would you be more comfortable with that?"

Giancarlo didn't look open to compromise, but he said tentatively, "Maybe that could work."

Oliver smiled. "I'll talk with Rahel."

Giancarlo didn't respond. He just stared at Oliver.

They stood feet apart, both nursing raw emotions and hesitant to reach over and forgive. Oliver realized it was one thing to feel that your partner didn't like something about you or that affection or passion might wane. But his paternal instincts had kicked in. Giancarlo's hesitancy in accepting Luca's special abilities and identity was unforgivable. It was a breach Oliver felt might be difficult to repair. For the first time in their relationship, he pondered the possibility of a rupture, a parting of ways, a divorce.

Giancarlo felt angry and embarrassed. He didn't agree with Oliver, but he recognized Oliver's capacity to think creatively and embrace novelty and, at some level, wished he had the courage to do the same. He had grown to appreciate his own preference for convention and the conservative financial world he inhabited.

He feared Oliver was getting caught up in the fantasy world of his son and that the two of them would grow increasingly unconventional. He couldn't imagine his cousins, colleagues or sister warming to them. Would they become isolated and shunned even more so than as gay men who had married and fathered children? He loved Oliver and his heart raced when he looked into his blue eyes and rubbed his hands through his wavy blonde hair, but right now, all he felt was distance and resentment.

Both Oliver and Giancarlo feared they would be unable to rekindle their affection and reach toward the other, the hurt deep and tender. Oliver's eyes watered and Giancarlo melted. He always thought Oliver was stronger, more resilient, but the vulnerability he saw on his husband's face moved him. He reached his hand toward Oliver's face and stroked his cheek, pressing his finger in the place where a dimple appeared when he smiled. Oliver began to sob. Giancarlo embraced him.

"*Amore, mi dispiace. Ti voglio bene.*"

"I love you, too. I'm sorry for our disagreement," Oliver echoed Giancarlo's words and sentiments. "We'll get through this, won't we?"

Giancarlo nodded, now choked with emotion. He cleared his throat and murmured, "I'm not as brave as you."

"I'm not as brave as I might look," Oliver said with a tentative smile.

"What are we going to do?" Giancarlo asked.

"What did our fathers do? They shunned us. I want to hate them and repudiate them. But, in the end, they were simply frightened. They didn't have the information that would help them make sense of us. They couldn't imagine a normal, happy, and rich life for us.

We're in the same place. We don't understand Luca, and we are afraid he will not be happy. Let's take it a step at a time."

"How did you get so wise?" Giancarlo whispered.

"You make me want to be the best I can be," Oliver replied.

Giancarlo leaned toward Oliver and kissed him. They both breathed each other in, letting go of the walls they had been building. Giancarlo gave Oliver a strong squeeze, embracing him solidly. Oliver felt Giancarlo's power, one laced with affection and gentleness. As brave as he might seem in the face of Luca's journey, he needed Giancarlo's support and perhaps that's all Giancarlo needed to know, that Oliver looked to him for strength and wisdom.

Giancarlo took Oliver's hand and led him into the bedroom. "I think you need to know how loveable you are."

He pushed Oliver onto the bed. He kneeled on the floor against the mattress, wedging himself between Oliver's legs. He unbuttoned Oliver's pants and let them fall to the ground, pressing himself closer to Oliver. He rubbed his hands on Oliver's thighs. Oliver arched his back in delight.

Oliver let go of his doubts – of the reservations he had about being able to get past disagreements with Giancarlo. As Giancarlo made love to him, he felt as if a spell had been cast, almost as if a power or force had taken hold of them, making it possible to get past seemingly insurmountable barriers. Oliver was emboldened and inspired and hoped he and Giancarlo could grow together in this new adventure.

15

Chapter Fifteen – Magical Curriculum

A week later, Oliver was sitting in Rahel's parlor, recounting his conversation with Giancarlo and the idea of Oliver coaching Luca.

"I think that's reasonable. I can see his reticence, and if this will enable us to help Luca, I'm all for it."

"What can you teach me that I can teach him?"

"Well, I have to say, this is a pioneering situation – not just for you and Luca, but for me."

"In what sense?"

"We're embarking on a unique path. Most psychics have never had formal training. They spend most of their lives denying, concealing, or fearing their gifts. Eventually, they can't ignore who they are and begin to embrace their abilities. Imagine a world where kids are taught to trust their spiritual gifts."

"What kind of gifts are you talking about?"

"There are all sorts – intuition, imagination, premonitions, clairvoyance, clairaudience, mediumship, healing, concealment, time travel, and the ability to weave new spells."

"Wow!"

"Yes, and that's the short list."

"How do we know what Luca is gifted in?"

"We're lucky that he's still young and not self-conscious about his abilities. They will be obvious if we pay attention."

"He definitely has premonitions."

"Are they premonitions or intuition?"

"What's the difference?"

"You mentioned he knows when his grandmothers are about to call or when someone is arriving at the door or when your husband is coming home."

Oliver nodded.

"These are not so much premonitions as his picking up on something that is happening, but others haven't noticed yet."

"Ahh," Oliver said.

"What about someone who has an accident – like choking?"

"If he is aware of something before it occurs, before it is even in process, then that is a premonition."

"He has great imagination – like changing weather."

"Yes, you've mentioned that. I believe he may be a weaver, someone who can create change and create new spells through imagination. It's a powerful gift."

Oliver raised his eyebrows. "And what about past lives?"

"What about them?"

"Well, Luca seems very connected to a particular past life."

"Yes. I've been wondering about that. Some people become aware of a past life's content, but others can travel back and forth between the past and present. The ability to be present in distinct moments is a form of time travel. It wouldn't surprise me that with Luca's intuition and premonition, he can move back and forth across time."

Oliver looked concerned, and Rahel noticed. "Don't worry.

We're not going to train him to travel in time. But if he has the gift, we want him to make sense of it when it happens."

Oliver's look of concern didn't dissipate.

"The most important lesson is to help young people trust their intuition or perception. Their spirit or higher self will guide them if they are willing to listen. Our rational ego-based society encourages us to discount our vibes or feelings in favor of a logical cause-and-effect world. If we can get Luca to trust his intuition, the rest will flow."

Oliver and Rahel strategized about some ways to help Luca, and a few days later, Oliver decided it was time to test some of the ideas they had come up with. Giancarlo was at the bank, and Francesco was upstairs taking a nap. Oliver was sitting at the table where Luca was coloring.

"Luca, do you want to play a game?"

He nodded yes.

"Can you tell me what color crayon I have in my hand?"

Luca looked curious, closed his eyes, and said, "Orange."

Oliver opened his hands and let the orange crayon roll back and forth in his palm.

"Excellent. You have very good intuition. Should we try it again?"

Luca nodded.

"What color do I have now?"

Luca closed his eyes and then said, "Green – but a light one."

Oliver grinned and opened his palm. A light green crayon rocked back and forth between his fingers. He whispered under his breath, "Amazing!"

"Let's try something different. I'm going to draw something."

Luca looked toward Oliver, who then interjected, "Don't look. Pay attention to your own drawing."

Oliver drew a heart in red. He looked up and said, "Okay, Luca.

Can you tell me what I drew? Close your eyes and trust the first thoughts that come to your mind."

Luca closed his eyes. He then began tentatively, "It's red. It's like a circle but isn't a circle."

Oliver held up his drawing, and Luca grinned. "A heart. I was going to say that."

"Why didn't you?"

"I wasn't sure."

For the next thirty minutes, they continued to practice the same kind of intuitive guesses. Luca was accurate about 70% of the time. He felt dejected when he missed a guess, and Oliver reminded him it was like exercising. You get stronger and better the more you do it and trust it.

At some point Luca said, "Dad, Francesco needs a change."

Oliver thanked him and went upstairs. Francesco was stirring and whining. Oliver smelled his diapers and, sure enough, he needed changing. He changed Francesco and brought him downstairs. He grabbed a bottle from the fridge, warmed it, and then sat with him at the dining table while Luca continued to draw.

"Luca," he said. "Granny Rita mentioned you told her you knew Francesco before."

Luca didn't look up from his coloring book, but he nodded.

"Can you tell me more?"

Luca seemed hesitant. He colored more aggressively.

"Is something the matter?"

"Did something happen?"

Luca nodded.

"Tell me."

Luca paused and then said, "Francesco saved me."

"How?" Oliver asked.

"He didn't like me, but he saved me."

"How?" Oliver asked again.

"It was dark, cold, and wet. He had a key. He opened the gate."

"Then what happened?"

"We hugged. He took me back home."

"Where?"

Luca nodded his head back and forth, struggling to formulate words.

"That's okay. You don't have to answer."

Luca continued coloring. Francesco sucked on the bottle and kept his attention focused on Luca.

A few days later, Oliver was sitting with Luca, and they were reading a book. Oliver put the book down on his lap and asked Luca, "When you tell me your brother is waking up or needs a change, how do you know that?"

"I don't know," Luca answered.

"Is there a voice – like one from God - telling you something?" Oliver decided to venture into the god language territory.

"It's both a voice and a picture."

"Who do you think the voice is?"

"Someone who can see Francesco and me at the same time."

"Ahh," began Oliver, "maybe that is God."

Luca nodded unconvincingly.

Oliver continued. "God is someone who connects us all. God is love. God is light. God is a friend who walks with us and is there to support us."

"Like you and papa?"

"Yes, but God is everywhere."

"Sometimes I feel like I am in more than one place," Luca said, looking up at Oliver.

"What do you mean?"

"Well, sometimes I'm here reading or coloring, and I can see Francesco."

"You can actually see him?"

"Yes, I can see him move or cry or smile."

Oliver wondered if this wasn't just Luca's imagination – a gift of being able to visualize what he was sensing, or perhaps just a form of creativity that happened to be true to life. He remembered leaving his book on Francesco's bed when he went up to check on him. He asked Luca, "Can you tell me what is on Francesco's bed?"

"His pillow, his favorite blanket, his teddy bear, and the book you were reading earlier."

"Bravo! I thought I accidentally left the book upstairs." Oliver rubbed his chin, amazed at how powerful Luca's abilities seemed to be. He was both excited and anxious, convinced he had a very special son and anxious that Luca's powers could be used for good or bad. He decided to test him further.

"Luca, can you see what papa is doing at his desk in the bank?"

Luca looked off into the distance and then turned back to Oliver. "He's not at his desk."

"Do you know where he is?"

"He's at the corner café having an espresso with another man."

Oliver took out his phone and texted Giancarlo. "Are you at the café with Riccardo?"

Giancarlo texted back, "Yes. How did you know?"

"Luca told me."

"What?"

"Yes. Luca told me. We've been playing some games, and his ability to visualize a place is uncanny."

"Wow!" Giancarlo said to himself. The realization that Luca had seen him was frightening. Riccardo was a colleague at work, and as far as Oliver knew, Riccardo and Giancarlo worked together and would, occasionally, go get a coffee together. After their fight the other night, Giancarlo began to look at Riccardo differently. Maybe he would be a good back-up plan, someone he could pursue should he and Oliver face barriers they couldn't overcome.

Giancarlo's heart raced. He quickly texted Oliver back, "That's amazing. You must be doing a good job coaching him." Deep down, he realized he would need to be more careful.

"Luca, you're right about papa. He was there with Riccardo, one of his colleagues at work."

Luca nodded, but he didn't smile.

Oliver decided to test Rahel's theory that Luca was also a time traveler. "You mentioned you and Francesco didn't like each other at one time. Where did you live?"

Luca looked over at his brother in Oliver's arms. He then closed his eyes and recounted, "It was a very big house with a large garden in the center. There were several carriages inside the garden area. Francesco was painting a large ceiling – so high it felt like it was the sky."

"What did you do?"

"I was in charge of books. There was a room full of books. I used to help someone read the books."

"Can you tell me who you helped?"

Luca closed his eyes again. He seemed to struggle. Oliver said, "Relax. Describe colors or shapes or impressions."

Luca began, "He's a man who wears red. He is serious. He likes to read and discuss. We sit at the table and read books together."

"Who is he?"

Luca nodded no. As he nodded, he seemed sad.

"Did you like him?"

Luca nodded yes.

"Did he like you?"

Luca seemed to struggle. "I wanted him to. But he liked Francesco more."

"How did that make you feel?"

"I didn't like Francesco, but I like him now." He looked over at his brother and grabbed his tiny fingers, giving them a little tug.

"Is the man in red here, too?"

Luca nodded no.

"Are you sure?"

He nodded yes. "He's gone. But you look like him."

Oliver murmured under his voice, "Oh my god. I wonder if Henry was somehow related to Salviati, perhaps a reincarnation of him?"

"Luca, once you told me you knew your way around this house. Did you live here before?"

He nodded yes. "The man in red and I lived here, then we went to the big house."

Oliver decided to test Luca a bit more. He asked in present tense, "What are you and the man in red reading here in the house?"

Luca closed his eyes. He said, "It's a book with different letters. I can read them, but he can't."

"Can you read them aloud to me?"

Luca had his eyes closed and mouthed some words in Hebrew. Oliver couldn't make them out but recognized the language. Luca spoke tentatively.

Oliver reached for a book at the side table that included Hebrew inscriptions alongside English and Italian. "Luca, what lettering is the book you're reading with the man wearing red?"

Luca pointed to the Hebrew letters.

"Bravo. It sounds like you are reading Hebrew. Can you read this?" Oliver said, pointing to the passage in the book he was holding out to Luca.

Luca looked at it and furrowed his brow.

"That's okay. Don't worry," Oliver said to him.

Luca focused on the passage and then tentatively said, "*Sh'ma Yis-ra-eil, A-do.*" He struggled and then said, "*Nai E-chad.*"

"Are you reading that, or did you memorize it?"

Luca looked bewildered.

"Can you point to the word *Adonai*?"

Luca pointed to the correct word.

"Very good, son."

Luca smiled proudly.

"Do you want to take a walk?" Oliver suggested to Luca. Oliver needed to take a break from the intense interaction and assumed it would be good for Luca too. Oliver went upstairs to the bedroom and dressed Francesco in a warmer set of clothes and put him in a sling around his chest. He returned, and they went to the front door. Oliver grabbed Luca's light jacket and cap and put them on him. He slipped on his own light jacket, and they walked down the stairs and out onto the street.

"Which way do you want to go?"

Luca pointed to the left.

"We'll follow you," Oliver said.

Luca grabbed his father's hand and walked down the street. Their house was near the convergence of three lanes. Luca took the one heading southeast. They followed its curve and meandered through several other lanes. Oliver was amazed that Luca seemed to know where he was going. Around a corner they happened upon a gelateria and small café. "Do you want some gelato?"

Luca nodded enthusiastically.

Oliver ordered a cup of hazelnut gelato for Luca and an espresso for himself. The sun was shining in the small square. Oliver leaned back on the wall and savored the feel of the early spring sun. He looked across the space and noticed an old building. It looked like a city government office with people going in and out with papers in hand. He had never noticed the structure before and walked over and read some plaques on the wall. Luca followed him.

It was currently a city permitting office. Previously, it had been a school. But as he continued to read, his heart skipped a beat. In the 16th century, it had been an institute for women run by an order of religious women. Oliver looked at Luca to see if he had any emotional reaction to the building. He was avidly digging a spoon into the cup of gelato, oblivious to his surroundings.

When Luca had finished his gelato, Oliver said, "Do you want to go inside?"

Luca nodded no and clung to Oliver's pant legs as if in fear.

"Ok. Do you want to go home?"

Luca nodded no and dragged his father toward the Capitoline Hill. They emerged from the dense neighborhood onto a busy boulevard, walked toward the ramp leading up the hill, and ascended, enjoying the unobstructed views of the city. Luca always enjoyed the site, staring up at the colossal statues of Castor and Pollux, and watching people ascend and descend the ramp.

Later that evening, they were all gathered for dinner. Francesco sat on Giancarlo's lap. Luca was in his special, raised chair, and Oliver went back and forth to the kitchen, bringing food to the dining table. Once seated, Oliver recounted the games he and Luca played.

"How do we know they aren't just lucky guesses?" he asked in a whisper, so that Luca wouldn't hear. Luca was engrossed in eating his risotto.

"Statistically, it's more than luck. And what about his knowing you were at the café?"

Giancarlo nodded nervously. He leaned over to cut some chicken on Luca's plate. "So, Luca, did you and daddy go out today?"

He nodded without looking up. He looked at Giancarlo's hand cutting his chicken and seemed upset.

"Papa, your finger."

Oliver looked over and noticed a band aid wrapped around Giancarlo's forefinger.

"What happened?" Oliver asked.

Before Giancarlo could answer, Luca said, "There's still a piece of glass under the skin."

Giancarlo looked at his son in disbelief. He looked up at Oliver and said, "I dropped a glass at work and, when I picked up the pieces, I cut myself."

Luca nodded.

"Did you get everything out?" Oliver inquired.

"I thought so, but our son seems to think I didn't."

"Let me see," Oliver commanded, getting up and walking toward Giancarlo. He pulled back the band aid and looked at the puncture in the skin. There was a small red irritated spot underneath. He rubbed his hand over the area, and Giancarlo recoiled.

"Ouch!"

"I think there's something still in there. Let me get some tweezers."

He returned with a magnifying glass and tweezers and examined Giancarlo's finger. He poked around and found a sliver of glass, pulled it out, and then pressed the wound with a small paper napkin. He wrapped it with a new band aid, and they continued to eat.

"Well?" Oliver interjected.

Giancarlo turned red in the face. He realized that there was little explanation for his son's ability to know how he had hurt his finger or that there was still glass in it apart from some extraordinary ability. He stared at Luca, but was unable to make the emotional leap to embrace the information.

"Pass the wine, please," he said in reply.

Oliver smiled, holding the wine in the air in anticipation of some declaration.

"Luca, I'm proud of you."

Luca smiled.

Oliver passed the wine but scrutinized Giancarlo's face as he poured another glass and looked down evasively at his plate. His husband was still unconvinced.

16

❧

Chapter Sixteen – Etienne

Oliver, Luca, and Rahel climbed the marble stairs to Etienne's home. Rahel had the grimoire carefully wrapped and nestled in a canvas bag. Oliver held Luca's hand. It was a cold day, and they were bundled in winter coats, scarves, and hats.

Rahel knocked on the door, and Etienne opened it immediately, as if he were already at the door in anticipation of their arrival.

"*Benvenuti*," he said warmly, waving them into the bright apartment. "Rahel, it is good to see you again. You are glowing as usual. And Oliver, thanks for agreeing to meet. And this must be Luca," he said, extending his hand to the boy.

Luca was uncharacteristically guarded. He glanced up at Etienne without a smile. He extended his hand in a shake, but withdrew it quickly after contact. Etienne noticed the reticence and tried to divert attention, reaching for Rahel's coat. "Let me take that for you," he said, helping her with one of her sleeves.

Oliver helped Luca pull his coat off and then slipped his off as well. Etienne took them to a small side room and returned. "Some tea, coffee, juice?"

"I'll have some tea," Rahel said.

"Luca, do you want some juice?"

He nodded no.

"I'll have coffee if it's no trouble," Oliver interjected.

Etienne retreated to the kitchen, and Rahel and Oliver strolled around the room, admiring the books on the tall shelves. Oliver continued to hold Luca's hand.

Etienne returned to the salon with a tray. He placed cups on a small table in the center of some easy chairs and poured Oliver's coffee and some hot water over a tea bag in a porcelain cup for Rahel. "Please, make yourselves comfortable."

"Etienne, you are looking good. You must be keeping busy," Rahel said, breaking the awkward silence.

"Well, I try. Between serving on several archaeological boards and gathering with friends, time passes." He took a sip of tea and then continued, "As I mentioned to you on the phone, I'm curious about what you could discover about the grimoire."

Oliver leaned forward on the edge of his chair and began, "Rahel has been very gracious. We were able to make sense of a lot of the book, but there is still more to learn and study. Besides the basic text, there are a lot of commentaries, as you know. It will take some time to complete our study."

Etienne nodded and murmured, "Hmm, hum."

"What Oliver is insinuating, Etienne, is that we need more time with the grimoire to do it justice."

Etienne leaned back in his chair, crossed his legs, and took another sip of tea. He glanced off in the distance and then looked back at Oliver and Rahel. "Let's move beyond pleasantries and get to the point. Where you able to decipher the text?"

"What do you mean?" Rahel asked, clearing her throat.

"Rahel, we've known each other for a long time. Let's be honest. I know you discovered that the text conceals itself. Were you able to read it with some help?" he asked, glancing furtively at Luca.

Rahel cleared her throat and said without elaboration, "Yes. We did."

Oliver interjected, "The book is amazing. The cumulative wisdom in the commentaries around esoteric passages, symbols, and spells is extraordinary. It appears to belong to a lineage of gifted individuals. As you mentioned to me before, certain books seem to find their way to individuals in mysterious ways. You thought this one was meant to find its way to me, and you were right. It was intended for Luca."

"How did it work?" Etienne asked excitedly.

Oliver and Rahel looked at each other, not sure who would take the lead and how much they wanted to divulge. Oliver looked at Luca and said, "Well, Luca is 5. It wasn't possible for him to read the text, but with his presence and permission, Rahel could read it."

Etienne's eyes widened, and he looked over at Luca, who remained quiet and emotionless.

Rahel leaned forward and said, "Etienne, why do you think the book was passed on to you, but you couldn't read it?"

He turned red in the face. "I've been asking myself that for a long time. My mother died when I was young, so I don't know if she could read it or not. I certainly embraced the arts, and I sought to learn everything I could to become proficient in magic. As you see, I have a vast collection of grimoires and other esoteric texts. But this one eludes me. I don't know why."

Etienne put on the best face possible, but he felt embarrassed and ashamed that he had not been able to penetrate the text. He had trained with the best wizards of France and Italy. He was considered an expert in esoterism, sought after by countless groups to lead conferences and give talks. He felt as if the grimoire mocked him and put in question his authenticity and his heart. He wrestled with a fundamental question: why was he not worthy?

Over the years, he had grown more comfortable with the concept of past lives and wondered if he didn't have a connection with the grimoire. Perhaps he had taken it from someone or sought to suppress it, burn it, bury it. If so, it's possible he and Luca had some karmic debt to resolve. He had traced the lineage in the back of the book and wondered if there might be some connection with Bishop Carafa who became Pope Paul IV. He bristled that he might have been someone as despicable as Pope Paul IV in a past life.

Luca's legs rocked, and a grin formed on his face. Rahel and Oliver both noticed. Oliver had rarely seen his son take delight in someone else's inadequacies, and he never saw him do so with an adult. He wondered what unspoken truth Luca had sensed.

Etienne continued, "I've concluded that it doesn't belong to me. As much as I treasure it, I feel like I must give it up. All I want is that it goes to the person who can open it. That is who it belongs to." He looked over at Luca.

Luca's grin morphed into a simpler smile, one that almost seemed compassionate.

"I would be happy to buy it from you," Oliver offered.

Etienne waved his hand dismissively. "That's unnecessary. Nor would it be right. I don't need money, and if it belongs to someone, it's not right for me to profit from it. I want to make sure it's in the right hands, and it would appear this young man is its rightful owner."

Etienne looked over at Luca, who continued to rock his legs and observe the adults calmly.

"Can you read it for me?" Etienne asked Luca.

Luca looked nervously at Rahel and said, "She can."

"Luca, can you come over here and sit on my lap? Why don't we read something to Mr. Brome?"

Luca leaped up from his seat and climbed onto Rahel's lap. She pulled the book out of the canvas bag and placed it on her lap. "Luca, why don't you open it up for us?"

Luca opened the book and turned several pages, resting on a particular one. Rahel immediately recognized it as one of the pages she and Luca had read before. There was a notation from LR in the margin. Rahel read the central passage that was written in Hebrew. She translated it as she pronounced the words in Hebrew. Etienne leaned forward in amazement.

The passage recounted elements of creation and the role of imagination in bringing the world into existence. It emphasized that as humans are the imagination of God and share in God's imaginative faculties, human beings have similar abilities to shape reality through imagination or, as the text suggests, through what is typically referred to as magic. LR's commentary relates the reticence of the Cardinal to accept this given the growing hostility to magic in influential circles of Catholic leadership. She believed he and other thoughtful leaders could see the reasonableness of natural magic, but feared their assets and benefices would be seized if they were accused of sorcery. She mentioned their fear of Bishop Carafa and others like him. She believed this was an egregious form of intellectual dishonesty.

At the mention of Bishop Carafa's name, Etienne's face turned red.

Rahel noticed.

"But aren't things changing?" Oliver postulated, trying to interject some hopefulness. "The scandals of sexual misconduct in the Church have diminished its moral authority. People are beginning to think for themselves and forge alternative forms of spirituality. Maybe this is precisely the time to revive the scholarship that was taking place in the late 1400s and early 1500s in Florence and Rome. This is more than a sorcerer's grimoire of spells. From what I have seen so far, the book is a rich exploration of the theology and philosophy behind spiritualty, mysticism, and human faculties for imagination, intuition, and creativity."

"If what you say is true, and I am encouraged by the optimism you express, your son is poised to play a significant role. The book and its teachings are only opened by someone who is part of the lineage. Obviously, your son is part of that. You have a unique role in nurturing that," Etienne noted.

"But I can't do it alone. I have no background or expertise," Oliver stated.

"But we do," Rahel added. She looked over at Etienne. He nodded.

"Oliver, I'm sure this is all overwhelming to you and, if you are a good father, you are bound to be anxious for your son, for his wellbeing," Etienne added.

Oliver nodded thoughtfully.

"I never had children," Etienne elaborated. "When I was your age, being gay was dangerous. The idea of living with another man or having a family was out of the question. I have a small fortune, and I am getting older. I would like to make sure that my wealth is used wisely."

Oliver's face turned emotionless, and he took hold of the arm of his chair tightly in anticipation of what Etienne was about to say. He looked over at Rahel and then back at Etienne.

"I would like to leave my estate to your son, to Luca," Etienne said solemnly, gazing intently at Luca.

Oliver felt blood rush to the surface of his skin. Etienne's generosity surprised him and wondered if there was a catch, if Etienne's motives were not duplicitous. "That would be very generous of you, but I assure you Luca is well positioned for his future."

"I realize that. You and your husband are well off. You will face unexpected expenses in the future, and I want to make sure Luca has everything he needs for his education."

Oliver worried that Etienne's statement was more than just a general remark about contingencies that everyone faced – that perhaps he had foreseen something. He was nervous that there would be some expectation on Etienne's part such as his having more interaction with Luca in the future. As much as he sympathized with Etienne's struggles as a gay man and a sorcerer, he seemed creepy, and he wasn't sure he wanted Luca to spend time with him.

Rahel could feel Oliver's apprehension and interceded. "What do you have in mind?" she asked Etienne.

Etienne shifted in his seat nervously. "I'd like to set up a trust."

Oliver rubbed his chin pensively. That didn't sound problematic. He wanted to ask if there were any conditions, but he didn't have to. Rahel could read his mind.

"And what kind of conditions might you envision?" she asked Etienne.

"Only two," he began matter-of-factly. "I'd like the trust to be set up at your husband's bank, with him serving as the trustee."

"And?" Rahel asked.

"And that you both agree to engage someone to mentor Luca?"

Oliver didn't consider those to be onerous conditions, but he expected Giancarlo would be more reticent. He said, "That is very generous of you. I'll need to discuss this with Giancarlo."

"Of course. I wouldn't expect anything else. In the meantime, consider the grimoire yours – or that is – Luca's. I hope you and Rahel and Luca can continue to study it. While it may be quite esoteric, your son seems ready to digest it – sooner than later."

Rahel breathed a deep sigh of relief. She knew Etienne could be irritable and quirky. He seemed extraordinarily reasonable and at peace.

"Oliver, I'm always at your disposal in terms of translations or guided readings with Luca. If you want to strategize more about lessons, we can do that, too."

Etienne smiled and said, "I hoped that if you engage someone, it might be Rahel. I've known her for many years, and she is competent and conscientious."

"I have the same impression," Oliver added. "She's been marvelous."

Rahel smiled, and Luca grinned at her warmly.

Abruptly, Etienne said, "Well, my friends. I have a meeting to attend to in a little while. Oliver, let me know what Giancarlo thinks. I'm happy to meet with him to answer questions or to formalize the trust."

Etienne stood. Rahel and Oliver followed suit, with Luca leaping off the chair onto the floor, rubbing his hand over the grimoire. Rahel leaned down, placed it carefully in her bag, and handed it to Oliver. "This is yours to keep safe."

Oliver nodded. He extended his hand to Etienne, who reciprocated with a warm handshake. Etienne and Rahel embraced. Etienne squatted down and shook Luca's hand. Luca smiled warmly as their hands touched.

17

Chapter Seventeen – The Seer

A week later, Giancarlo, Oliver, and Luca were riding up the gondola at Courmayeur. The sun was shining on the fir trees that passed their window. A few clumps of snow rested in the branches, but it was clearly spring. The pistes to town were thin and, when they arrived at Plan Checrouit, there were more people sunning themselves on the terraces than skiing.

They exited the first lift and walked to the second. As the doors closed and the cabin lifted over the runs, Oliver looked toward Mont Blanc and the ridge of snow-laden peaks. "It's so beautiful," he said to Giancarlo.

"I never tire of it. What a change of scenery from Rome!" Giancarlo added.

"Are you ready for a day on the slopes, Luca?"

He nodded as he played with his gloves and helmet.

"Any more thoughts on Etienne's offer?" Oliver pressed Giancarlo, taking advantage of Luca's fascination with the slopes below.

"I realize it would be nice to have those funds – both for Luca and for me at the bank. But I'm still uneasy about it. Don't you think it's odd that someone you just met a few weeks ago is offering his fortune?"

"Not really. It happened when Henry left me his estate. Come to mention it, in both cases, you are the managing trustee."

Giancarlo looked evasively out the window to hide a grin. He then interjected, "You said before that you thought he was a little creepy."

"Yes. He's eccentric. I'm sure you've met others like him in Rome – old, rich, gay, single."

"I've met single gay rich men, but I don't recall any of them being sorcerers or wizards or whatever you call him."

"Do you think they would disclose that to you?"

"Probably not," Giancarlo admitted. "But I'm not sure I want to agree to mentoring Luca in the so-called arts," he whispered, hoping Luca was still engrossed in managing his ski gear and didn't over-hear him.

The gondola arrived at the terminus station. They walked out into the bright sunshine. Luca dragged his skis behind him as they made their way to a small level area where everyone was stepping into skis and pushing off onto the slope below.

"You ready?" Giancarlo said as he looked down at Luca, who had stepped into his bindings. He looked like he was poised to head down the mountain.

Luca nodded. Oliver adjusted his goggles and put the straps of his poles around his wrists. All three shoved off onto the freshly groomed run. Giancarlo skied aggressively ahead of them. Oliver held back. Luca headed straight down, making quick turns left and right.

They reached the bottom of the main trail. "Very good, Luca! You remembered what you had learned last time we were here!" Giancarlo exclaimed.

Luca nodded proudly, surveying his surroundings.

They caught a chair lift that would allow them to ski to the other side of the mountain. They took a series of runs on the north side of the resort in the shadows of a major chain of peaks separating Italy from France. Luca skied well, and Giancarlo and Oliver enjoyed the change of pace and scenery from Rome.

Giancarlo texted Maria to check in on Francesco. He held up the phone to Luca and Oliver when she texted a photo of Francesco back.

"He's so cute," Oliver remarked as he enlarged the photo on Giancarlo's phone. Maria had purchased some new outfits and was having fun playing godmother.

Luca peered at the photo and creased his forehead. "What's that?"

"What?" Giancarlo asked.

"That red mark."

"I don't see anything," Giancarlo said. Oliver peered at the photo but didn't notice anything either.

"What are you seeing?" Oliver asked his son.

"There's a red mark on his arm."

Neither Giancarlo nor Oliver noticed a red mark. Giancarlo texted Maria back. "Luca thinks he sees a red mark on Francesco's arm. Do you notice anything?"

"No," she texted back.

Oliver didn't want to invalidate Luca's observations or intuition and said, "Thanks for pointing that out, Luca."

He nodded proudly.

They pushed off on another run and made their way back to the other side of the mountain, where they planned to meet Pietro for lunch after his morning lessons.

At Plan Checrouit, they secured a table at the edge of a terrace overlooking the valley below. They enjoyed a pleasant lunch with Pietro who, Oliver thought, looked even more handsome than during their trip at Christmas. Pietro and Giancarlo caught up on old times, and Pietro promised to bring his partner to Rome in the spring when they both had some downtime.

Toward the end of their lunch, Giancarlo received a text from Maria. "Not to alarm you, but when I was changing Francesco, I noticed a bruise on his arm and another on his hip. I don't know how that happened."

Giancarlo replied, "Maybe he bumped himself against the side of the crib."

"It's padded," she texted back.

"Monitor things, and if it gets worse, let me know."

"*D'accordo.*"

Giancarlo, Oliver, and Luca skied another couple of hours and then headed back down to Dolonne to rest up and have dinner.

While at dinner, Maria sent another text. "The bruise has gotten larger. And there's another on his other arm. I'm going to take him to the doctor."

"Oliver, Maria is going to take Francesco to the doctor to look at the bruises. Should we go back?"

"Let's wait to hear what she finds out."

Giancarlo nodded, and Luca looked concerned.

A few hours later, Maria texted. "I think you guys may want to come back early. The doctor is concerned. They are going to run a series of diagnostic tests, but he is worried it might be a genetic blood disorder that can present itself this way – with bruises."

Giancarlo shared the information with Oliver, who agreed they should return to Milan right away. They packed their bags, checked out early, and drove to Milan. Maria was still at the hospital with Francesco. Giancarlo dropped Oliver and Luca at Maria's and then went to the hospital.

"Oh Giancarlo. I'm so worried," Maria said in a panic as she embraced her brother.

"I'm sure it's nothing," he tried to reassure her.

"He's so fragile and innocent," she said, tearing up.

"They'll take good care of him."

Giancarlo went to the nurse station and inquired as to the status of his son. They assured him he was being monitored carefully, and that diagnostic tests would be back tomorrow. He returned to Maria and said, "Why don't you go home? I'll stay with him here."

"I don't know if I can sleep."

"At least you will be at home and can have something decent to eat. I'll keep you posted."

"I'm going to stay here with him. Why don't you go back to Oliver and Luca?"

Giancarlo nodded. Reluctantly, he returned to Maria's apartment, where Oliver and Luca were watching TV. Luca ran to his dad and gave him a hug.

"How's Francesco?" he inquired.

"He'll be fine. The doctors are taking good care of him," Giancarlo assured him.

"Did they see the red marks on his back?" Luca asked.

Giancarlo creased his forehead and looked at Oliver.

"Yes, they did," he said to assure his son, although neither he nor Maria had seen anything on Francesco's back.

Luca smiled but then returned to his state of concern.

"They will take good care of him, and he will be well and come home soon," Giancarlo assured him.

Luca didn't seem convinced. Oliver noticed and said, "Luca, why don't we get ready for bed?"

He nodded, took Oliver's hand, and followed him into their room. Oliver said quietly, "Thank you for noticing the red marks today on Francesco. No one else did, but you did. Always trust what you see."

Luca was quiet.

"Are you worried about Francesco?"

Luca nodded.

"Why don't you give him a hug in your mind? He will feel it and that will make him better."

Luca closed his eyes and imagined himself hugging Francesco. Oliver noticed his body twitching as if in an embrace. Finally, he opened his eyes back up and crawled into bed. Oliver tucked him in and turned off the light. He returned to the parlor, where Giancarlo was sitting pensively.

"So, what do you think?" Oliver began.

"Maria said the doctor thinks Francesco might have a genetic blood disorder. They're running tests to determine what might be the case. There are several types of maladies, and they respond well temporarily to blood transfusions, but later require a bone marrow transplant," Giancarlo explained.

"Would that involve Luca?" Oliver inquired.

"If he's a match, yes.".

Oliver rubbed his chin in thought. "By the way," he said to Giancarlo, "did you think it was odd when Luca said something about red marks on the picture Maria sent us earlier? I saw nothing."

Giancarlo creased his forehead and said with some consternation, "I know. It was uncanny. Maybe we just missed it."

"Open your phone," Oliver said to Giancarlo. "Scroll to the photos Maria sent."

"Here," Giancarlo said as he made the photos larger, scrutinizing them for a mark.

"Do you see any red marks on Francesco's arm?"

He nodded no.

"But later in the day, bruises appeared, right?"

He nodded.

"Luca mentioned them before they appeared. That's amazing."

"Tonight, he asked if you had seen the marks on his back and you said yes, right? But you saw nothing."

Giancarlo nodded.

"We have a son who has premonitions or sees things in advance. This is not ordinary childhood imagination."

Giancarlo looked off into the distance. "It's been a long day. I think I'm ready for bed."

Oliver nodded, and they walked into the bedroom.

"Oliver, I think I might be ready for Rahel to mentor Luca," Giancarlo interjected unexpectedly.

Oliver detected Giancarlo's anxiety about Francesco's condition. He could feel his heart beating quickly.

"He does seem to have a gift."

Giancarlo nodded. "I have to admit that this incident pushed me over the edge."

"It's scary, isn't it?"

"I don't want to lose him. He's so fragile," Giancarlo remarked, referring to Francesco. He sobbed, and a few tears streaked down his face.

"We won't lose him. He's got good medical care. I also sense there's some karma between Luca and Francesco, and Francesco's illness will be a defining moment – for the good."

"I sure hope so."

"So, should I talk to Etienne and Rahel?"

"The sooner the better," Giancarlo said uncharacteristically. He was clearly interested in soliciting any and whatever help he could to save his son.

"I'll call both tomorrow. Now, why don't we get some sleep?"

"I don't know if I can sleep."

Oliver pulled Giancarlo close to him and held him snugly in his arms. He kissed his shoulders tenderly and said, "Just relax. We're in this together."

A few moments later, Oliver could hear Giancarlo's deep breaths and knew he was falling asleep.

18

Chapter Eighteen – Carlo

Oliver and Giancarlo took the train to Milan with Francesco and Luca. Maria was excited to see them all. Luca was growing up so quickly. He was conversational and curious, and Maria enjoyed reading with him, chatting, and taking walks. Francesco was doing well, although everyone was on alert to periodic bruising and other complications. He, like Luca, was a charmer.

Maria wanted Oliver and Giancarlo to meet Carlo, someone she had been dating. After Francesco's birth, she took the initiative to speak with the guy she had been eyeing at the coffee shop. He seemed ideal – a lawyer, never married, and quite comfortable with the alternative family she had with Oliver and Giancarlo. He was smart, affable, affectionate, and adored Maria.

Maria called Oliver and Giancarlo to do a gaydar audit. She thought he was straight, but she wasn't certain. Carlo dressed well, had a meticulously clean and ordered apartment, had a lot of gay friends, and knew all the best clubs and restaurants.

Maria organized a party with several colleagues from her law firm, friends from the neighborhood, and Carlo. Luca and Francesco were with a sitter down the hall in her building, and Oliver and Giancarlo helped Maria set out the food and drinks. Carlo arrived early. Giancarlo's heart skipped a beat when he walked in the door. He was far more handsome than Maria had described. He was tall and lanky, but in a sexy sort of way. He had a large, sensuous nose, a broad forehead, dark wavy hair, and a beautiful jaw and chin where a hint of late-day stubble gave him a certain allure. He had a long powerful neck that plunged into a loosely fitting cotton shirt, opened loosely at the top.

He was affectionate with Giancarlo, knowing that he might be his future brother-in-law. Giancarlo took Carlo's touches to be more than just the Italian propensity for touch, and wondered if Carlo might not, in fact, be gay.

As other guests arrived, Giancarlo grew disappointed. Carlo showed the same affable and affectionate demeanor towards others – men and women, apparently a signature feature of his personality. Maria approached and said, "Well, what do you think?"

"Of what?" he replied.

"Of Carlo," she said, sighing.

"He's adorable. He seems very self-confident and friendly. Look at him. Everyone loves him."

"I know. It's that way every place we go."

"Are you okay with that?" Giancarlo asked his sister, wondering if the asset might become an annoyance at some point.

"Absolutely. He makes everyone feel at ease and feel as if they are special. I like that about him."

Another guest approached Maria. "*Maria, che bella festa! Mi piace Carlo. E tuo cognato è molto simpatico.*"

"Yes, Oliver is wonderful, and I'm glad you like Carlo. *Questo è il mio fratello, Giancarlo.*"

"*Giancarlo, questo è Antonio.*"

"*Piacere,*" they both said as they shook hands.

Antonio stared into Giancarlo's eyes. Maria noticed and gulped. "Antonio, Giancarlo is a financial advisor, like you."

Giancarlo raised one of his brows. They began to visit. Maria excused herself.

"Your sister is wonderful. We met at some mutual friends' house. I'm glad to finally meet her big brother," he said, as he glanced up and down Giancarlo's torso.

Giancarlo blushed.

"So, you're a financial advisor in Rome?"

Giancarlo nodded, mesmerized by Antonio's powerful presence. He was not particularly tall, but there was something very sensual about his large head, round face, thick, closely trimmed beard, dark hair, brown eyes, and muscular frame. He had brilliant eyes and a cute mouth. He gestured with great animation and had a gregarious smile.

Giancarlo nodded distractedly. He took a sip of his wine, looking over the rim of the glass at Antonio. "Are you with one of the banks here in Milan or on your own?"

"I work with a financial advising firm. If you ever consider moving to Milan, we're always looking for talented people."

Giancarlo blushed.

A man approached them. "*Ciao, caro,*" he said to Antonio as he gave him a kiss.

"Giancarlo, this is Eduardo. Eduardo, Giancarlo."

"*Piacere,*" they both said. Eduardo looked more northern Italian – light hair, fairer skin, tall and thin.

"Eduardo is Carlo's cousin."

"Ah," Giancarlo said. "Carlo and Maria seem to be getting along nicely."

"Yes. I guess we're all here to meet him and check him out," Antonio said.

"I have known Carlo for years. He's affable, but definitely not gay," Eduardo remarked.

"Good to hear. She's enamored with him," Giancarlo added.

"I met Oliver. He's a dear. I hear you guys like to ski. We have a group of friends here who ski often. You'll have to come with us sometime," Eduardo said warmly.

"That would be great, although we just introduced one of our sons to the sport – so we're likely to be skiing as a family."

"That must be fun," Antonio said unconvincingly.

"He's so cute."

Antonio nodded. "Next time you're in town, we'll get a group of friends together."

Giancarlo looked around the room, a cross section of Milan social life – urban, professional, and mostly gay. He surmised he and Oliver were the only full-time parents, perhaps even the only married gay couple. He imagined their lives – his former life - dinners out, parties on the weekends, and journeys to nearby mountains for skiing. He and Oliver were looking forward to parent-teacher conferences, quiet dinners at home, and now, lessons in magic and psychic things, he thought to himself with chagrin.

Eduardo excused himself and wandered across the room to another set of guests. Oliver was engrossed in a conversation with one of Maria's friends who, Giancarlo learned, was a co-parent with a gay couple. She was their surrogate and, like Maria, involved in the child's life. They were exchanging parenting stories.

Antonio seemed like he was about to excuse himself, and Giancarlo placed his hand on his upper chest affectionately and asked, "So, I imagine the financial world in Milan is more open than in Rome – I mean in terms of gay advisors and clients."

"Yes. It's a non-issue here. In fact, at the bank, we have Christmas parties for our clients. It's almost as if one had stepped into a gay bar."

"I can only imagine," Giancarlo said with a chuckle.

"They would be eating out of your hand," Antonio remarked, glancing up and down Giancarlo's well-sculpted torso.

"We have to be so careful in Rome. And now, with the kids, there's an added complication."

"I can't imagine. Kids are cute, but I don't think I'm parenting material."

"I didn't think I was either," Giancarlo remarked, "but you do what you have to do."

Antonio looked restless, so Giancarlo quickly added another line of questioning. "Where do you ski?"

"Courmayeur is one of our favorites. Lots of cute ski instructors!"

Giancarlo thought of his handsome friend Pietro and chuckled.

"Listen, I have to go say hello to someone. I'll be back in a little," Antonio said, placing his hand on Giancarlo's forearm.

Giancarlo extended his hand warmly and stared into Antonio's eyes. "It was nice to meet you." Their gaze lingered, and Giancarlo realized he had crossed a line. He glanced over at Oliver, still engrossed in his conversation.

Giancarlo wandered toward Carlo, who held Maria close to him. "Carlo, how are you holding up with this crowd?"

"It's a great party," he said, looking proudly at Maria. She beamed.

"We're glad to meet you finally!"

"I'm glad to meet you and Oliver. I've met the kids. They're adorable."

Giancarlo nodded.

"Carlo mentioned we should all go skiing with them sometime," Maria noted.

"You ski?"

Carlo nodded.

"He's being modest," Maria said. "He's an excellent skier. I think he'd be great with Luca – and, eventually, Francesco when he learns."

Giancarlo felt the blood drain from his face as Carlo mentioned

Francesco and skiing. With his condition, he wasn't sure he'd be able to take part in sports where bruising was a distinct possibility.

"I hope Francesco can ski without problems," Giancarlo said with deep concern.

"He will. It's just a matter of time when they will find the right treatment or be able to do a marrow transplant."

Giancarlo nodded, looking at Maria with alarm. He felt so conflicted – at one moment his paternal instincts kicking in and in the other, his longing to be a carefree, gay man joining friends for parties and weekends out of town.

Carlo excused himself, and Maria stayed with Giancarlo. She looked inquisitively at him.

"He's not gay," Giancarlo said emphatically. "He's perfect for you."

"I think so," she said with a warm smile. "I'm glad you like him. He likes you guys and, as he mentioned, adores the kids."

Maria got pulled off to the side by one of her friends, and Giancarlo went to the bathroom. As he pushed the door open, Antonio was heading out. "*Scusa*," Giancarlo said.

Antonio didn't step out of the way. Instead, he stared into Giancarlo's eyes. Giancarlo advanced, thinking Antonio would step aside, but he didn't. Instead, he leaned into Giancarlo and gave him an extended kiss on the lips. "*Scusa*," he echoed Giancarlo's earlier statement and smiled sheepishly.

Antonio then stepped aside and left the bathroom. Giancarlo went in, peed, and returned to the party. He eyed Antonio from across the room. Antonio grinned. Giancarlo glanced at Oliver, still intently discussing parenting with the lesbians. As Giancarlo pivoted, he realized Maria had been watching him. He wasn't sure what she had seen, but he was nervous.

Later that evening, Maria, Carlo, Oliver, and Giancarlo sat down after they had cleaned up, and debriefed, commenting on the various guests and their idiosyncrasies. "Everybody loved you," Oliver said to Carlo.

"I didn't realize I was on trial," he replied.

"You weren't, although this was the first time many of us had met this mysterious man Maria kept talking about," Oliver noted.

He blushed.

Maria turned to Giancarlo. "What did you think?"

"Of Carlo?" he asked, already knowing that wasn't the question.

She glared at him.

"Your friends are wonderful. They seem like a nice network of professionals who enjoy life here in Milan. It's definitively less conservative than Rome."

"Oliver?"

"Your friends Matteo and Franco were nice. It was great meeting another couple who have a child."

"I'm sorry I missed having time to speak at length with them," Giancarlo remarked.

There was an awkward silence when Carlo interjected, "We'll have to go skiing sometime. Antonio and Eduardo love to ski. And I believe Sofia and Carla ski as well."

Giancarlo nodded. He looked at Oliver. "What do you think? Would we bring the kids or leave them with someone?"

Oliver looked as if Giancarlo had two heads. "What do you mean? Of course, we'd bring the kids. Luca is becoming quite the skier." He looked at Maria for support. She nodded, but glanced at Giancarlo.

Giancarlo was feeling increasingly tied down, domesticated, and the conversation was only emphasizing the ambivalence he felt during the party. His gay life was over. He was a parent and husband and banker. How boring could one get?

Oliver noticed the regret on Giancarlo's face and made a promise to address it later.

The four of them continued visiting. Oliver went to the neighbor down the hall to get the kids, who were already sound asleep. He tucked them into bed and waved Giancarlo into their adjacent bedroom. "We have a long day tomorrow," he reminded him.

Giancarlo nodded, gave Carlo and Maria kisses on the cheek, and retreated to his and Oliver's bedroom.

Once the door was closed, Oliver walked up to Giancarlo and kissed him passionately. He grabbed the back of his head, pulled him close, and opened his mouth wide, the two of them sharing the warm wetness within. Oliver ran his hands up and down Giancarlo's firm torso, squeezing his muscular pecs through the fabric of his sweater.

"I kept watching you tonight," Oliver began. "You are the hottest guy in the room, and I am so lucky to be with you."

Giancarlo wished he could have said the same thing. He merely nodded. Yes, Oliver was exotic – his blonde hair, blue eyes, and dark complexion were striking. He was young, athletic, and full of energy. But the image in his head continued to be Oliver chatting with other parents, undoubtedly discussing school, day care, and sports.

Oliver's psychic work with Luca had honed his own intuition, and he could feel Giancarlo's reticence. He pushed Giancarlo toward the bed and pressed him down on the mattress, unzipping his pants and pulling them down. Giancarlo became aroused, and Oliver took hold of Giancarlo and stroked him. Giancarlo moaned.

Oliver realized that, besides Giancarlo's fear of becoming too domestic, their lovemaking had become routine and predictable. He unzipped his own pants and let them fall to the ground. He stood over Giancarlo and decided to spice things up a bit.

Thirty minutes later, after bringing Giancarlo to the brink several times, they finally climaxed and collapsed in each other's arms. "Wow!" Giancarlo exclaimed. "Where did that come from?"

"I've been thinking, I don't want us to take each other for

granted. I love being a parent, but I don't want to forget that we are gay men and there's a whole community out there we should cultivate relationships with. We should go out for drinks, dancing, skiing, and to the beach in the summer. Sometimes we can bring the kids, but sometimes we should enjoy being us."

Giancarlo smiled. "You always amaze me," he said, without elaboration.

Oliver knew he had narrowly pulled Giancarlo back from a dangerous point. He also knew he would have to do more.

The next morning, the sun was barely up, and Luca walked into the room holding Francesco's hands, helping him walk. They climbed into bed with Oliver and Giancarlo. Luca put his arms around Oliver, whispering in his ear. "*Madrina* is making pancakes!"

"*Oh si? Allora, Andiamo.*"

He turned to nudge Giancarlo to wake for breakfast, when he noticed Francesco crawling up on his chest. Giancarlo was making faces at him. They rubbed noses and Giancarlo gave Francesco a warm hug. Giancarlo gazed at Oliver and gave him a reassuring smile.

Oliver leaned over and gave Giancarlo a kiss. He grabbed hold of Francesco and lifted him into his arms. He, Luca, and Francesco walked toward the door on their way to the kitchen. Giancarlo glanced at them and realized how fortunate he was. He had just made love to and slept with an incredibly sexy man, and he had two adorable children. How many of his gay friends would trade all the party nights in the world for what he had?

19

Chapter Nineteen – Motherhood

A Year Later

"Maria and Carlo, smile for the camera!" Giancarlo said as the happy couple turned toward him after giving each other an enthusiastic kiss. Everyone applauded.

"Franco, can you let the waiters know we're ready for dinner?" Oliver suggested as he ran after Francesco, who was running toward the rose garden.

Sonia, Franco's wife, gathered her kids and got them settled at the table overlooking the countryside and the Via Appia Antica. It was a beautiful day for a wedding.

Piero, Giancarlo's other cousin, clenched his wife Angela's hand. He was still uncomfortable around Giancarlo and Oliver and their kids, and only reluctantly came to the ceremony out of respect for Maria. They had also grown distant from Franco and Sonia over their support of Giancarlo and Oliver's family.

Giancarlo walked up to them with Luca holding his hands and said, "Piero and Angela, you're both looking good. It's been a long time."

Piero nodded. "We've been busy. Between Angela's new business and the kids – well, we just don't seem to have much time to socialize."

"Glad you could make it. I know it means a lot to Maria."

"So, she's moving back to Rome?"

Giancarlo nodded. Oliver walked up to him with Francesco in his arms. "Piero and Angela. Good to see you!" he said.

Angela kissed him on his cheeks; Piero nodded coldly.

"Yes," Giancarlo continued, "Maria's moving back. A firm here in Rome has hired her and Carlo. We're delighted, and so are the kids."

Piero glared at Giancarlo as if to say, 'She should have been with them all along.'

"Maybe we can all get together at the villa in San Felice Circeo. It would be nice to share some time at the beach."

Angela said, "That would be nice." Oliver detected her insincerity.

Everyone sat at a large common table set under the vine-covered pergola. The waiters brought bottles of mineral water and red and white wine. Giancarlo made a toast and soon thereafter, the waiters brought out ceramic dishes filled with spinach pasta noodles coated in a tomato and cream sauce with a small square of slightly charred cheese on top.

"They're called *scrigni*," Giancarlo explained to Oliver. "Little chests."

"Hmm," he said as he took a bite. "Delicious. Why haven't we been here before?"

"I don't know. This place and this dish used to be a favorite of my parents. Maybe I avoided the memories."

Later, the waiters brought trays of mixed grilled meats and an assortment of vegetables. A soft breeze blew up from the hillside. Oliver detected the light aroma of freshly plowed fields, wildflowers, and a hint of old masonry, perhaps from the many archaeological sites nearby. The entrance to one of the most important catacombs in Rome, St. Sebastian, was just across the roadway.

Sonia leaned forward across the table and asked Carlo, Maria's husband, "So, what do you make of this group?"

"What can I say! I'm thrilled. I never thought I would be part of a family like this."

Sonia looked perplexed. Maria admonished her with her eyes not to press for more information. Carlo had grown up with an abusive father who used to beat his mother and verbally belittled him. His mother died when he was in college, and he never returned home to his dad. He was afraid he had inherited his father's demeanor, so he avoided dating and never wanted to father children.

However, he fell madly in love with Maria. Their relationship blossomed in the months after Francesco's birth, and Carlo realized he didn't have an abusive bone in him. That Maria already had children was a relief to him.

When Francesco was diagnosed with his blood disorder, Maria decided she wanted to be more involved in parenting Luca and Francesco. It delighted Oliver and Giancarlo that she wanted to move to Rome. Luca still called her *madrina*, but Francesco called her *mama*.

"Where are you going to live?" Piero inquired.

"We found a place near Giancarlo's and Oliver's place. It's not far from our work, and we can spend more time with the boys."

Piero didn't look pleased. The idea that Francesco and Luca would have three fathers and a mother unsettled him.

"How does all of that work?" Piero pressed further.

"I'm not sure I understand your question," Carlo replied, knowing full well that Piero was insinuating that this would confuse the kids.

"Where will the kids stay?"

"We have a bedroom for them in our place, and they have a bedroom in Giancarlo's and Oliver's place. It's more like households of old where there were multiple generations and families living together sharing in the parenting of children. The so-called nuclear family is a very modern invention. We think Francesco and Luca will benefit from a more extended and rich family."

Piero glared at his wife, who took a long sip of white wine.

Oliver had Francesco on his lap and gave him a small piece of chicken to chew. He ran his fingers through Francesco's dark hair and placed several errant strands back in place. Francesco was enthralled with the large family gathering and couldn't take his eyes off the many aunts, uncles, and cousins gathered around him.

Francesco had responded well to a recent round of transfusions. He had grown up quickly, trying to keep up with Luca. He had already acquired an extensive vocabulary for his age, and he was particularly expressive, smiling intently at people around him.

Maria was beaming and wondered if she might not become the matriarch of the family as she looked around the table. She was the oldest, but had always retreated to her professional life. She felt more inclined to parent, and the idea of orchestrating large family gatherings was beginning to intrigue her.

Luca walked up to her side and gave her a rose he had picked from one of the nearby bushes. "*Ecco madrina. Auguri!*"

"*Grazie, Luca.* It means so much that you are here for my wedding! You've become such a handsome and talented young man!"

"And you're going to live near us here in Rome?" he asked, seeking confirmation of the news he heard earlier.

"Yes. I will be just down the street. We will have a room for you. You can come anytime you want."

Luca smiled broadly and ran back to Giancarlo and hopped up on his chair. Giancarlo gave him a squeeze and kissed the top of his head. Luca leaned toward his father and asked quietly, "Papa, why does Uncle Piero not like us?"

His son's question baffled Giancarlo. They had spent little time with Piero and Angela and, to his knowledge, neither had ever said anything disparaging to the children about their atypical family.

"Why do you ask?"

"I just get a feeling. Maybe it's the way he looks at you and dad."

"You're very observant," Giancarlo said to him, knowing that Luca was both very perceptive and highly intuitive and that it was important to support Luca's impressions.

Luca stared at Piero and Angela from across the long table and suddenly Piero knocked over his glass of red wine, spilling it onto Angela's white dress.

Giancarlo hugged his son and whispered in his ear, "What are you doing?"

"I'm making sure he won't hurt us," Luca said confidently in a low voice.

Giancarlo whispered to him again, "Luca, I think Piero and Angela are jealous of our family. They wish they had what we have – two fathers, a godmother, and now, a godfather. We don't have to be angry with them. We can help them know we love one another and that we love them, and hopefully they will see they have a beautiful family, too."

Luca smiled and breathed deeply. It felt good to let go of his apprehensions.

"So, you don't think they are angry with you?" Luca asked.

Giancarlo pondered how best to respond to his son. On the one hand, he didn't want to question Luca's intuition – he was clearly picking up on Piero and Angela's dislike of their family. He knew Oliver and Rahel were teaching him how to create protections for himself, to keep people from harming him or, as they tried to describe to Giancarlo, to keep people from disturbing or depleting his personal energy. Giancarlo appreciated Oliver's and Rahel's perspectives, even if he didn't entirely understand them.

"I don't think they want to hurt us," Giancarlo began tentatively. "I think they are afraid. We need to show them love."

As Giancarlo mouthed those thoughts, he realized what he really wanted to do was tell his cousin off, to tell him, *vaffanculo*, fuck-off. He was angry that people thought disparagingly of his family. He thought it was fascinating how raising kids forced him to reconsider his aggressive tendencies and foster more civil interaction.

Luca perceived his father's latent self-doubts and said, "Papa, you and dad are the best. I have the best family."

He leaped off his chair and ran toward Piero and Angela. Giancarlo grew alarmed but didn't want to cause a scene and watched carefully as Luca approached them. Luca said something to them, and they smiled. They looked over at Giancarlo, smiled, and nodded. Luca returned to Giancarlo, taking the long way around the entire wedding party, waving his hand as if he were a conductor of a symphony. He approached Giancarlo, who leaned down and took his hand.

"What did you tell Uncle Piero and Aunt Angela?"

"I asked them where my cousins were, and I told them when Carlo and Maria are back from their trip, we want to have them over for dinner. We miss them."

"What did they say?"

"They said they would like that."

"*Bravo!*" Giancarlo said. "Sometimes we have to protect ourselves from those who want to hurt us, but sometimes we just have to show them love since they are afraid." He was proud of how emotionally intelligent his son was becoming. Even at six-and-a-half, Luca was skilled at picking up on others' moods and states of being.

After cake and champagne, people sent Maria and Carlo off on a honeymoon. Everyone made their goodbyes, and Giancarlo, Oliver, Luca, and Francesco returned to the center of Rome.

Once inside their apartment, they tucked Luca and Francesco

into bed for a nap and went downstairs for some coffee. Giancarlo began, "Are you sure you are okay with Maria taking more of a role with our kids?"

Oliver nodded. "I can't think of a better arrangement. I think co-parenting with Carlo and Maria will be great."

"Are you sure? You know, it's been hard enough learning how to co-parent between us," Giancarlo said, raising one of his brows playfully.

"Once I wore you down, it was easy," Oliver said in retort, leaning into Giancarlo's side on the sofa and breathing in his manly scent.

"Seriously. You don't think it's going to make things more complicated?" Giancarlo asked further.

"I hope not. You never know. But Carlo seems like a very thoughtful and caring person, and Maria already has a good relationship with Luca and with us. We're all on the same page."

"Even regarding Luca?" Giancarlo pressed.

"You mean his gifts?"

Giancarlo nodded.

"I've always wondered about Maria," Oliver began.

"What do you mean?"

"Well, she has a lot of art that includes images of Minerva."

"Minerva was one of the prominent Roman divinities – part of the Capitoline Triad," Giancarlo remarked.

"But she's also considered one of the wise women associated with healing."

"Did she always have the artwork, or only after Francesco was diagnosed?"

"Always," Oliver said emphatically. "And she has bowls of rose quartz crystals and amethyst in her house."

"So?"

"I've always wondered if she was sympathetic to psychic things, to belief in energy work and spirits," Oliver said.

"I never noticed," Giancarlo remarked.

"That's why I'm not worried. She's aware of Rahel's work with him, and she seems okay with it."

"What about Carlo?" Giancarlo pressed further.

"That remains to be seen. But if he loves Maria, he's bound to be comfortable with her leanings."

Giancarlo nodded. "By the way, things seem to be going well with Francesco's treatments, right?"

Oliver nodded. "For the time being."

"Don't be pessimistic."

"I'm not. I'm being realistic. These transfusions only work for a while. At some point, we will need a marrow transplant."

"He's too young, now."

"Yes, but at some point, he will need one."

Giancarlo rubbed his chin pensively and stared off into the distance.

"Are we going to be okay?" Giancarlo continued.

"What do you mean?"

"Are we going to be okay with more interaction with Maria and Carlo? We're going to be less insular and private."

"I don't see that as a bad thing. They will not share our bed!" Oliver said with a grin.

"No. I'm the only one with access there!"

"Me, too," Oliver said as he brushed the front of Giancarlo's trousers. He could feel a slight hardness under the fabric and rubbed his hands over it again.

"Come here," Giancarlo said as he pulled Oliver close to him. "You are my family. You are what makes my heart pound and my pulse race. Never in my wildest dreams would I have envisioned a day like today – seeing my sister get married and having our children play with their cousins at the wedding dinner. It will only get better as our sons learn a rich poetics of love from the many people in their lives."

"When did you become a philosopher – and where did you pull that word poetics from?" Oliver asked.

"Think about it. So many kids grow up thinking there's only one model of family life and one way to be a woman or a man. Our sons will grow up seeing lots of different family types and see women and men sharing power and roles around parenting and partnership. It's amazing and wonderful!" Giancarlo said as he looked intently into Oliver's eyes. He gave him a warm kiss and stroked the back of his head. They undressed and slipped under the covers, snuggling close to each other. Soon, they were fast asleep.

20

Chapter Twenty – Karma

Two years later

Giancarlo, Oliver, Maria, and Carlo were at Bambino Gesù Hospital in Rome, meeting with the pediatric blood specialist Mateo. He was someone Giancarlo knew through his circle of gay friends. This made them all feel better about the sensitivity of the team toward their atypical family.

"As you know, your son Francesco has Congenital Amegakaryocytic Thrombocytopenia. We have minimized risks to him through periodic transfusions, but ultimately, he needs a bone marrow transplant if there is any chance for long-term survival. He's at the age where we can consider that."

The implication of what the physician said was overwhelming. Giancarlo's eyes began to water. Oliver reached over and held his hand. Maria held Carlo's hand.

"Your son Luca is a good genetic match. We need to have your consent about whether you are comfortable putting him at risk in being a donor for his brother."

They all looked at each other and Giancarlo said, "We've been talking, and we think this is the right thing to do. Luca has a close attachment to his brother, and we believe he would want to do this.

We've asked him, but of course, his comprehension of what is involved and the risks he would face is limited."

"Ultimately, you have to decide for him. Most donors do not have any trouble afterwards, but it is not an insignificant procedure, and there can be complications. And, of course, there are a lot of risks for Francesco. But without the marrow transplant, there are even more risks and long-term problems," Mateo explained.

"We're aware of all that," Giancarlo noted. "When would this take place?"

"The sooner the better. I can check schedules of the team, and we can then set a date. Do you have questions?"

Oliver inquired further as to the prognosis, the risks of the procedure for both boys, and recovery. After the consultation, they left the hospital and went back to Paola's to pick up both boys.

A month later, Maria, Carlo, Giancarlo, and Oliver held the hands of their boys as they were prepped for surgery. Francesco squirmed a lot, not happy with the portal for IVs. He wanted a hug. Luca put on a brave face and looked lovingly at his brother. Oliver held his hand. "You're very brave to do this for your brother," he said.

"I owe him," Luca said. Giancarlo creased his forehead and Oliver smiled.

Luca was now eight-and-a-half. The connection with his past life was not as unfiltered as it had been when he was younger. He was firmly rooted in his current identity and circumstances. But, since Oliver and Rahel had mentored him, he had grown to appreciate the lessons and insights he was bringing into this life and the unique challenges he faced, albeit an understanding limited by his age. He realized he owed Francesco something, and he was glad to donate his marrow.

During the operation, Giancarlo, Oliver, Maria, and Carlo paced back and forth in the waiting room. Oliver eventually suggested they take a walk. "I need to get some air," he said as he looked around the room at a lot of anxious parents.

Carlo said he would remain and text them if there was any news. They exited the hospital and walked a couple of blocks up the Gianiculum Hill. It was a sunny spring day, and the tops of the trees lining the Tiber River were greening up. In the distance, they could see the snow-capped peaks of the Gran Sasso behind the bluish-green hills of the Castelli towns. The city of Rome spread out before them, and Oliver kept thinking how surreal it was that it was his hometown, that his life in Boston continued to fade in contrast to the responsibilities of parenthood in Rome.

Oliver held Giancarlo's hand. Maria stood by, looking out over the city. Oliver said, "I have a good feeling about this."

"I don't know. They are both so young and fragile," Maria remarked.

"Aside from Francesco's condition, Mateo thinks they are both in good health and should do well," Oliver assured him.

"It's going to be a long recovery, particularly for Francesco," Maria remarked nervously.

Oliver nodded. "I've blocked my calendar for a while, and my moms said they would come help if needed."

Giancarlo took a deep breath. They walked farther along the ridge of the hill and then back to the hospital, stopping at the bar overlooking the city for a quick coffee.

Back inside the waiting area, Mateo came through the door with a big smile. He walked up to Giancarlo, Oliver, Maria, and Carlo and gave them each a big hug. "Everything went as planned. They are both recovering and doing well. Do you want to come be with them as they wake?"

They nodded. A while later, Luca woke first. His first words were, "How's Francesco?"

A tear streaked down Giancarlo's face, and he said, "He's doing very well. Thanks for what you did for him."

"We talked with each other while it was happening," Luca added.

Giancarlo looked at Oliver and Maria. Oliver looked at his son and said, "Tell us all about it."

"Well, after the bright light and the face mask, I went to sleep. But then I woke up and could see Francesco. He looked afraid, so I held his hand and told him it would be okay."

"You did well," Maria said, trying to hide her surprise at Luca's colorful description of the surgery. "And how did you do?"

"It didn't hurt. I could see them inserting some long needles into my bones. See here," he said, pointing to some bandages.

Eventually, Francesco stirred and woke. He whimpered until he felt Giancarlo's hand hold his. He closed his eyes and drifted back to sleep. The nurses came in and checked his vitals. "Everything looks good," one of them said to Oliver and Giancarlo. "It will take him more time for him to wake fully, and his recovery will take longer than Luca's."

They nodded.

A week later, Luca was reading a book, and Oliver was preparing dinner. Giancarlo called him on the phone from the hospital.

"Oliver," he began, panting. "Mateo says there's a problem. Can you and Luca come quickly?"

Oliver turned off the stove, covered some pans, and put a light jacket on Luca. They left the apartment and walked a couple of blocks to a taxi stand and headed for the hospital. Once there, they went inside, finding Giancarlo, Maria, and Carlo conversing.

"Francesco is developing a fever and a few other symptoms suggesting that he's rejecting the graft of Luca's cells," Giancarlo explained to Oliver.

Mateo came into the room and invited them to his office. He began, "As you know, Francesco is spiking a fever. We have given him additional drugs that suppress the rejection of the graft, and we will continue to monitor things. This is the point where things are touch and go."

"Is there anything we can do?" Maria asked, fighting back tears.

"No. I just wanted to share information with you and let you know what we are doing. I know this must be very stressful."

Giancarlo nodded. Oliver rubbed his chin, pondering what to do next. They thanked Mateo for his work.

Maria and Carlo agreed to stay at the hospital while Giancarlo and Oliver went to pick up Luca at Paola's and take him home.

"Oliver, I'm so scared," Giancarlo murmured.

Oliver took hold of Giancarlo's hand and squeezed it tightly. "Things will be okay. I think we might need to get Rahel and Luca involved."

Giancarlo shook his head. "It's too much of a burden to place on Luca. He's distressed enough about his brother."

"But maybe this is an opportunity for him to come to his aid. We know he can see things others can't, and he spoke to Francesco during the operation."

"That's what he said, but we don't know that for sure. If everything were fine, why are we at this point now?"

"I don't know, but what do we have to lose?" Oliver pleaded with him.

"Luca could become disillusioned if he can't make things better, assuming responsibility when it isn't his."

"Or it could work. We can explain to Luca that there's no guarantee, but we want to ask for his help."

Giancarlo began to cry. "I don't want to lose him."

"We won't. Let's think positive," Maria added.

Giancarlo nodded.

Later that evening, Giancarlo, Oliver, Rahel, and Luca sat in the parlor. Oliver explained that Francesco's body was having a difficult time accepting Luca's cells.

Luca nodded and then said, "He feels bad accepting my help."

"How do you know that?" Oliver asked.

"I can feel it. He still feels bad about our fight."

"What fight?" Oliver pressed.

"The fight a long time ago."

"You mean when he was an artist?"

Luca nodded. Giancarlo's forehead creased. He still found the whole notion of Luca's relationship with Francesco in another life impossible to believe or comprehend.

"Well, we need to convince him that you appreciate what he did for you, and now it is your turn to do something for him."

Rahel reached over and put her hand on top of Luca's and smiled encouragingly at him. Luca smiled and nodded.

"Can you close your eyes and visit him?" Oliver asked.

Luca nodded.

"Can you tell him you want him to get better so you can both play together?"

Luca nodded again, leaning forward in his chair. He closed his eyes, took a couple of deep breaths, and smiled. The adults sat quietly as they watched Luca extend his thoughts toward his brother. A few minutes later, he opened his eyes.

"And?" Oliver inquired.

"I gave him a hug and told him I loved him."

"What did he do?"

"He hugged me back and said he would be okay."

"That's good," Giancarlo noted hopefully.

Rahel then said, "Why don't you visualize your blood cells making friends with his body? Can you do that?"

Luca nodded.

"Blood cells are red round cells. Why don't you visualize them as hearts and send them into his body as expressions of your love?"

Luca closed his eyes, rested his hands on his thighs, and breathed deeply. His face was calm. His mouth formed a gentle smile. He kept that position for longer than the first effort to communicate with his brother. He eventually opened his eyes and said, "All of my hearts are in him now. They seem happy there, and I saw Francesco smile.

Giancarlo looked askance at Oliver and Rahel, worried this was just wishful thinking.

Oliver then said, "Let's make sure you have enough hearts for yourself. Close your eyes and welcome hearts from the universe into your own body."

Giancarlo rolled his eyes. Oliver glared at him. Giancarlo mouthed an "I'm sorry," and took a deep breath.

Luca closed his eyes and sat still for a while. A few minutes later, he opened his eyes again. "Dad, did you see the red bird fly over?"

Oliver looked at Giancarlo and Rahel. "You mean the cardinal?"

"Yes," Luca said enthusiastically. "He flew over us and dropped lots of hearts on us. I let them fall on me. They melted into my skin."

"Wow!" Oliver said, astounded that a connection seemed to have been made with the Cardinal, with Salviati. He held his son's hand and said, "Good work. You did a lot for your brother. Let's hope he gets better."

Mateo called later and reported that the fever was still alarmingly high, but he continued to hope the drugs they were administering would minimize his body's rejection of Luca's marrow. Giancarlo looked at Oliver and Luca and decided not to tell them. He held the disappointment within and put on a brave face.

The next day, he and Oliver relieved Maria and Carlo and sat with Francesco. He slept a lot, and nurses continued to check his vitals and tried to keep him comfortable. At one point, a physician and several nurses rushed in, looking alarmingly at the monitors and injecting him with something to bring down the fever.

Giancarlo felt resentful toward Oliver and Rahel for building up his and Luca's expectations. He sensed Francesco would not make it, and he worried it would devastate Luca. He held Francesco's hand and rubbed the inside of his palm tenderly. He prepared himself for the worse.

"Olie, I'm not getting a good vibe here."

Oliver, choked with emotion, walked toward him and held his other hand, both of them looking at their son. The rhythmic chirp and ping of monitors felt eerie, reminding Giancarlo of his father's death years before.

"What are we going to tell Luca?"

"We will tell him the truth. He did what he could to let Francesco know he loved him. That is what is important."

"But he's going to be so disappointed – mostly with himself."

"I know. Maybe it was a mistake to get him involved," Oliver admitted reluctantly.

Giancarlo glared at him but realized even having Luca become a donor raised expectations, and he didn't regret that they tried that. The visualization of healing and love only added to that and wasn't the sole source of disappointment.

"Why don't you go home and stay with Luca? I think he's going to need some support," Giancarlo suggested.

"I'm not sure I can leave."

"I know. But I'll text you if things get worse. Luca needs you."

Oliver reluctantly left the hospital, picked Luca up at Paola's, and took him home. As they walked toward their apartment, Luca asked, "Dad, why are you so sad?"

"I'm just worried about Francesco."

"He's going to be okay. I know it."

"That's okay, son. You don't have to be brave or put on a good face for us. We know he's in danger."

"No, he's fine."

Oliver looked at his son and could feel his determination. "How do you know?"

"I felt hot at Paola's. I thought I had a fever. I told her, and she felt me, and she said I was normal."

"What did you do next?"

"I knew I was feeling Francesco's fever and that he was still in trouble."

"What did you do?"

"My book says that you can do it with imagination. I decided to imagine the heat lifting from me. I visualized waves rising from my head."

"And?"

"Well, soon I felt cool. I think you should text papa and tell him Francesco is better."

Oliver nodded but felt odd texting Giancarlo, who was there in the room and able to see better than him. He feared he would get angry that we were just playing mind games.

Shortly, a text came in from Giancarlo. "Don't get too excited yet, but Francesco's fever seems to be coming down."

"Good news," Oliver texted back.

"How's Luca?" Giancarlo added.

"He's telling me how he visualized heat rising from him and from Francesco."

"Amazing," Giancarlo concluded his text.

"Well, young man, it would seem you are right on target with your intuition. Papa said Francesco's fever is lowering."

Luca beamed with joy.

A week later, Francesco returned home. Oliver took time off to stay with him, and eventually he regained strength and vitality.

"I'm relieved," Giancarlo said to him as they stood at Francesco's bed, watching him eat some gelato.

"Me, too. I wasn't sure he was going to make it," Oliver whispered to Giancarlo.

He nodded.

"So, what would have happened if he didn't make it?" Giancarlo began.

"What do you mean?"

"Well, I appreciate everything you and Rahel did to get Luca to visualize Francesco's recovery, but what if it hadn't worked? What if we had lost him? Isn't this all a matter of luck? We lucked out."

"You can look at it that way, and it certainly makes sense. There's no proof Luca did anything. It could well have been the medicines that prevented Francesco from rejecting the marrow."

"And if that's the case, why risk Luca's disappointment?"

"I've been thinking about that," Oliver began pensively. "Isn't the point in all of this that Luca can communicate love and affection for his brother? That his brother can feel love from Luca?"

Giancarlo nodded.

"Even if Francesco had died, Luca would have had the satisfaction of knowing he had done everything he could for him. He would know that he had paid his karmic debt and one way or another, Francesco would have known he was loved."

"But isn't that just a trick we play with ourselves? We find a way to see goodness even when a situation isn't good?" Giancarlo continued to press.

"That's one way to look at it. But, if we think of things from the perspective of God or the universe, what counts for good or bad? Isn't the essence of life to love and be loved? Our material possessions, bodies, and professions are the context for us to grow, learn, and love," Oliver explained.

Giancarlo sighed deeply, aware that indeed he and his sister had managed to heal from the punishing expectations of their father. He gazed at Oliver, who had made peace with himself and with his biological father, and who loved Giancarlo and their sons so generously. He observed Luca, who was affectionate and loving toward his brother, his parents, and his friends, and who had grown to appreciate his own gifts. And Francesco was now a healthy and happy little boy with a promising future ahead of himself. Maybe it was all about love after all. A group of individuals had finally come full circle, but Giancarlo imagined they still had more to learn. He was ready to continue the adventure.

The End (At Least for Now)

About Author

I am a Boston and Provincetown based author specializing in LGBTQ romance novels.

My fiction writing began twenty years ago when I was searching for creative ways to engage my college students in religion and ethics. I began working on a historical novel about Rome in the 1500s. The historical novel took shape around several key individuals – a cardinal, an artist, and a sorcerer. Francesco de' Rossi was an artist brought to Rome by Cardinal Giovanni Salviati, a Medici and prominent cleric pivotal during key events in Rome and Europe. The Cardinal employed a Jewish immigrant to translate manuscripts in his personal library. She happened to have been a sorcerer and inherited a grimoire (a book of magic) from her grandmother in Andalusia.

During the course of writing the book, I experienced a deep compulsion to paint. Over the years, I developed a parallel career as an artist. During the pandemic, however, I took up the pen again and began to write gay romance novels set in overseas locations. The writing was a way to travel in my imagination.

The gay romance novels weave together various threads of my life – my having lived in Rome for five years, my love of foreign languages, my interest in LGBTQ themes in the context of religion and culture, and my love of art, archaeology, and local cuisine. The narratives include rich characters who struggle with sexual identity and embrace new models of love and family. I include detailed descriptions of historical and artistic sites, illuminating their relevance for making sense of the past and inspiring personal transformation in the present. The stories explore new models of spirituality and religion. The books are page-turners with fast-paced plots, unique twists and turns, and intense sexual passion between characters.

The story of Francesco de' Rossi, Cardinal Giovanni Salviati, and Lucia Ruiz was finally incorporated into *A Roman Spell*, published January 2022. The book is a sequel to *Oliver and Henry*.

For more information on published and forthcoming books visit: www.michaelhartwig.com

CPSIA information can be obtained
at www.ICGtesting.com
Printed in the USA
BVHW041152020222
627885BV00012B/211

9 780578 364520